Letter to Another Human Like Me

& other fables & stories

By H.D. Moe

Beatitude PRESS

BERKELEY, CALIFORNIA

Book and Cover Designed by Douglas Rees

Printed in the United States of America
By Beatitude Press, Berkeley, California

ISBN: 978-147-822-8820

Contents

Lucy & the Longhorn

HEN LUCY'S Oldsmobile broke down on the country road, needing assistance, she limboed under an electric wire & after a mile or so, winnowing between bramble bushes, there looked to be an opening into a pasture. Something drew her on. At dusk she seemed to be pushed toward the big cow standing across some barely visible path. His horns seemed to wink to her. She thought it was by the hope of a farm house near, yet what forces were they that like one dumb thickening wind were crazily magnetting her along? Something not known shaped an inhibiting question within, becoming lassooy as it grew now around & around & duplicating itself, loops coiled her very sinews. In this mummified state of doubt mixed with fear, she thought, who could move? Then, just after both their poised figures, eyeing each other, commingled together with this deepening darkness into a giant shadow asterisked with starlight, Lucy heard rhythmic thuds from the ground as the bovine approached. It was totally dark now, she could smell the large animal's grassy breath puffing on her face. Nether moved. She felt like a heart of hot fudge waiting to melt the ice cream starry mind it was moored in, so she could run, run, run away from this invisible beast. Whereto? As she remembered, before the almost completely moonless black set in, a wild forest surrounded the path. Limbs to poke out her eyes, ravines to fall into? The large beast stepped back & pawed the hard dirt with his hoofs. Her pulses penduluming with the thunder in her ears, Lucy mimed her body still as a stone. Again, the longhorn approached up close.. She lowered her breathing to a tiny fog on the mirror of her now precarious mental control. Suddenly, Lucy could no longer hold back the hurricane of fear & doubt whirling within her & she screamed at the bull & the night: "GET OUTA HERE"! The animal turned around, she could feel the brushing wind of his horns & then it trotted back a few yards, stopped & turned around again pawing the ground. Since, it seemed, he couldn't make her out in the dark enough to charge, Lucy became calmer. She turned & knelt down quietly & lengthering her body along the narrow path, began slowly pulling & hunching herself away from the bull with her knees, feet & elbows like a broken snake. At first, she heard nothing but the shuffling whispers of these peristaltic movements along the ground. Then, after, it seemed, only two or three minutes of crawling, Lucy's heart stopped, the

giant bull started following her. A minute passed & the bête noire was panting above her heels. Even though she quit moving her body parts altogether, Lucy wondered, 'will he hear my breathing & my heartbeats now thumping against the ground & trample me with his hoofs like he would a snake? No, quiet yourself down, maybe he was bored with his life as it was lately & curious, maybe he just wanted to play, charge at some target.' All this immense nocturnal unwordable event surrounding & within her was way beyond her or anyone's understanding Lucy felt. She became a radical agnostic that moment. After playing possum for what it seemed to be an eternity, the cow slowly plodded a ways off. 'I hope he turns into a Ferdinand addicted to wild flowers perfuming the air now somewhere & leaves me alone', Lucy thought, as she, quietly as possible, flipped over on her back & looked up at the stars.

LETTER TO ANOTHER HUMAN LIKE ME

UGGED BY FAIRIES, I can overhear the spheres on the jute box of the poli-universe what came around always new turned back to its makings & invented it anew too. Nothing remains the same. Different empty shapes appear though for those, who enjoy these protean abysses, contemplating a quiet between the wiry traffic, the sudden floods of sentiment rushing through. These underlooking animisms show their glow from any part of me that isn't clothed & rays shoot out mathematical angles of my body so that I may not disrobe myself in the presence of anyone it seems for they always think my flesh is nuclear, I'm the devil, an invented zombie or I have arrived from another planet than this one, or some such nonsense. Even shaking hands or hugging anyone becomes impossible unless I cover myself completely like a traditional Muslim woman. Whenever I leave my hut I carry in a knapsack, a hooded robe, mask & gloves to don when I reach the outskirts of the village. The other creatures who visit me & I meet along the way, are not put off by my glowing rays at all, in fact, they cheerfully greet me on my walks through the woods & console me with their songs, chirps & voices, at down-in-the-dumps times I feel from being rejected by my own kind. Earlier, I wished that the fairies & their emanations would leave me, but now I would feel greatly impoverished if either the magical winged ones inside me or their rays & glows did go, in spite of the resulting alienation I suffer from being shunned & vilified by my fellow human beings. Not only am I continually enlightened by the deep gossip humming & musically proclaiming throughout my listening brain, all matter of friendly phantoms, duppies, elves & tricksters from the past, future & everywhere now, it seems, are drawn by these emanations & along with the birds, bears, panthers, foxes & hares (to name a few) they talk & gesture to me wonderful strange but true informations. Did you know that truth is not in the idealizations of demonstrative & experimental science or any known discipline? Truth is the unknowing that's always new. It's not even in what I'm or rather the fairies, ghost creatures & animals are saying here. It could only be whatever it is, in the vast intimacy of you & the creative poli-universe or maybe coming novelly from some whiteheadian creative baby god or goddess at the nub & circumference of everywhere always. I don't know & am not being told by these cogent posits swimming up to & throughout me. If I

do get even an improvised guess, I'll tell you or whoever's open to my inklings. Meanwhile, hidden in the midst of unnecessary biases & hardships & the wars resulting from this lack of caring vision, sequestered in my little cabin deep in the forest here, away also from the prominent robot-like thinking of my species, although without the companionship & love of another human, awash with intelligences of nature & illuminating, loving, numinous spirits of the real nether world, I'm happily jumping to an undefeated dance.

To Be Or Not to Be, Is This the Question?

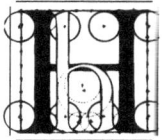ARRIET had to find a traveling place where neither he would ever visit, nor surmise that she might appear, not the opposite either of either of their haunts, for in order to escape Dean's obsession, all permutations of mutual reasoning must be eschewed. His multitude of masks she knew blended & came apart into single goal-focused roles like a kurtosis curve according to no self within him & she was the only target now. The moon grew above her into a giant Cyclops eye of white light, as she sprinted toward an imagined randomness, oddities too little to hide her alleycatted from betweens, novelty cried at a distance intimately insane, then superman's phone booth flying by offered to give a lift to Harriet's needed elevator of awakened dreams. No, she felt, as its talking door jaw-dropped & tromboned into an orgasmic web of receding stars. Some secrets were left for her to uncover. What hadn't she told Dean or herself in the year of their revealing? Yes, their transference & counter-transference was a total osmosis, yet she was left with something, the something he existentially must have in the seeking at least to be alive. Not even nothing could be more impoverished than what he was lost in alone. She could feel her crowded heartbeats widen as the cool dawn arose, rays dabbing touches on Harriet's sweating face. Passing the public square, thoughts of securing a restraining order entertained her thought, though who could identify one with no self? Shape-shifters who replaced their body parts like whims in an infinite kindergarten? Mental athletes with the emotionality of a shot putt? All was responsible as nobody was. Shades loomed up like overhanging King Cobras, simultaneous with the ascending, blazing daylight, while Harriet jogged along the edge of an abandoned grave yard, remembering what Dean had told her, that he wanted to die but couldn't. Some flux out of mysteries' control would not let him be. After that last session with Harriet when he seesawed into her on the wings of an angry dove, alighting upon the bottom (he told her later) where every bounce is, finding through his own discovery & invention then, birth & death, the makings of the sources & the sources of each making, Dean possibly would embody a singularity. Yet once he came out again with what he hoped was a shibboleth in this outside abyss & there being nothing but nothingness within his terrible everlasting life, what escape was left but a plunge into her flesh & soul. Yes, she could feel then that the good

husband, the one that could be & do everything, supervening as a Zulu chief in a sea awash with virgin brides conniving through her waving veils of aliveness for Harriet's pregnant buddhahood. Oh, this trapped psychopathic, solipsist now, had glimpsed an inkling of the wonderful other & it was her, his watchtower ticket onto happy freedoms' rocket ship. 'Didn't he know he was running to become elected God while already the incumbent'? Harriet sentenced in her desperate mind as she traipsed slowly up the winding road to The Institute Of intelligent Genetics A009. Maybe they had the genome of his manufacture, if, as she suspected, he was a total human simulacrum or had he been engramed at birth for a rebirth? The question of whether Dean had any humanness or 'Who' in him or was he anything at all, which she had never pondered before, dragged her tired body higher & higher along the winding pavement like a fishing hook. Once inside the underground building of the Institute, light blue outfitted from head to toe, attendants, escorted Harriet to the records department. Since she was still officially married to Dean, access to his file, if there was one, was open to her. She finger-spelled out his full name: "Laurence Dean Zitternick" on the computer modicum. Nothing appeared on the screen except a notice "did not match any documents". Furthermore, links to all natural births, golemizations, Trans-humanoids, Servo-Automatons or new-myth-genetic creatures within the inner galactic network of required origin identity came up with nothing too. Dean must have either deleted himself or to have been by somebody erased from official existence altogether. Why? As she was being escorted back out of the underground building, Harriet noticed the returning way was not following the same route as she had come in along. She was about to question one of the attendees on this, when on turning a corner, there, to Harriet's horror, in a large tomb-like room sat Dean at the end of a long dark table aligned with partial & completely non-human beings. On a banner hanging on the wall in a large droopy smile in back of & over her husbands head, the proclamation: "CONGRATULATIONS TO DEAN ZITTERNICK FOR BEING REINSTATED AS THE CHIEF SCIENTIST OF THE INSTITUTE OF INTELLIGENT GENETICS", burned like a pen knife tattoo carved in the flesh of her mind. "Harriet, now don't be upset, I tried to enter your human world, that's why I was fired from the Institute, all out of my love for you. I've failed to be fully human & will never gain your humanness, I realize now. While I was trying to find you to be birthed, I thought, as at least the resemblance of a family man, I found in my research of all the living creatures in the multi-universe as we know it, you are the only one left capable of giving natural birth. All of nature's creations have gone extinct except you. I couldn't do it, but fortunately, of course, we have a sperm bank that will serve to get you pregnant, so we can continue, for a while anyway, an immediate line of the old human nature for our studies. Unfortunately, all the female producing X chromosomes in all sperm is gone, maybe, through some environment change, we don't know, so the upshot is, you will give birth to only male humanoids." Harriet faced him, trying to look as a meek & inquisitive child, while her anger toward this deceptive manikin rose within her. "Do I have a choice in this?" The big manikin or whatever he was, if he was anything, stood upright, towering over her, with a wide droopy smile on his made up physiognomy like the banner above them. "No, that won't be possible. You are our queen bee now.

CROWDED SOLITUDE

ISSY BEGAN out of a sum of Unthing, she thought, coughed up by the worst flag's laugh. From the get-go, jetting thumbs, dovetailing mind-ware, so it snowballed the awakening fields out of their philogenetic repertoire, mirroring Imelmann loops & then stalling still, which buzzed the Unthings into a discombobulating panic the most, seemed to be her proclivity. 'It's bad, I know, but its as far as I can tell, my only virtue', she felt her sailing wings signal. 'She was like the Raven, some Unthings pooled to calm the othering of the others, 'holding down a favored crow, defying its assemblage, until an estranged morph jogged near'. Her butterfly hands had, unbelievably to the Uns, broken away from their osmotic scaffolding, become detached from all topologies & holons, pinpointed in their wildly immediate focus. "We conjured her exactly", waved the Great Curved Flow, "What went down?" A surging ripple leaped a kniving: "The wind swirled too nicely through the jerry-rigged channels & I knotted no light even peaked a dim over our long vanishing rows of thought blossom." "& too", a rolling humped, "If her whims tickle to form the exogenous telepresences?" "Not more than a swoon of nows away, either" sloshed in a dip. "Hibernating in those potential walnuts we imagoed, damn!" cupped a swell. "& what will event when they believe again in the divine object?" bubbled up a foaming. "we'll be cut up, violated forever!" ooped a splash. "Now, now, don't be whipped up by these little mental breezes", The Big Curve, gellingly interrupted, "When a happening shapes, we'll golem it, like we always do. Our occasions of lapping will zombie any pretending thing that has the audacity to feel an encompassing edge." "Yet, why do we continue to mouth these happenstances into possible omnivorous delusions?" "Now she's losing her loyalty to us by the operative second." "This could be the start of an individuation plague." "Now, she's turning upon her now as a self-choosing everything!" kissed together an explosion of wavelets. Missy wheeled above the maelstrom belly-button, tucking in all around her in a funneling cone. "There she is, flying the air into differing shapes." "Like a blind envelop to be opened by who knows", two white tips peaked. Within the calm middle of the avalanche & volcanic eruption hour-glassing its yuga gyroscope inside & outside her between, Missy grooved in & out of whatever swam within her swimming, depending upon whether it was frightening or

not. A transparent loving godmother would suddenly become an opaque colossal desert spider eyeing her as its latest prey. 'Every happening unglued her gravity & must, in turn, form her attractive & escaping direction, she ruminated. Betwixt the open smile & the devilish tooth-flashing grin, cinnamon bear angels nested in the tree-crotch she flew through now, chased by the bicycling spheres of the Mystical One, the seas' dogged waves barking at her wing-tips for her Icarus blood. Missy could feel a surd neutrality, a clear agnostic Gnosis, 'no flow or one would ever be able to put a word or a hang on, for as soon as even a thought attempted to label this as a thusness, it poofed like the popped wink of a bubble', She waverly flexed in her motioning notions. 'Every smoking whisper I'm mirroring up my imaginary chimney pipe didn't reverse Old Saint Nick into a burglar of myths', she also noticed. For though, toying with her tortured Unthing childhood would only mothball her in an nostalgic heart not her own now, to them, her flaming wrote a message in the inkling night: "Glancing around me here & nowhere, you fuzzywuzzies of immediate tomorrows will always inform me where not to go". At that, all The Unthings in her vicinity seemed to vanish in the clearing that was trailing & leading her. The shiny dust layering Missy's immense monarch hands, as she alighted upon the rising radiant forehead of the blossoming sun, dostoevskied off its tiny windows, powdering the updrafts & lulls with such a blending of bands, like an uncurved vague rainbow, the horizon line of sky, land & water couldn't be distinguished & no thing, she knew, would ever lose its looking back.

MEISM CONFOUNDED

AT FIRST, when the algorithmic randomized system of health had taken over belief, almost everybody listened to their specific unconscious, then, yes, generalizations landed, cookie-cutting highways of the drifting mind, but these were nothing more than silver-lining whispers & blinks traversing the airwaves that the dwindling government philosophers turned onto. Brad awoke Melinda with a kiss. "Fuck mistakes", he echoed to the thought receiver. Translating laughs were sent. Love swamped fear here, yet Brad could imagine at the edges of his quiet emptiness, its peek-a-boo. As light enveloped them in warm morning sunshine & Melinda yawned like a lion at dawn, he saw descending upon him fires of embarrassment, breathless mirrors focused to kindle his wild homecoming. Looks diving into the soul of their total lives revisited, jumped thru humptydumpty peeps & yugas arose. Deaths died. Birth to birth communicated unprogrammed novella's flux & irony. Nevertheless, while Melinda found happiness in everything now, vibes gathered around him like wrinkles of a pruned-down nighttime. Not even my dreams can escape this longevity commune's surveillance, Brad knew without letting this awareness manifest itself in thought. He sunk into his familiar, until their velvety bones touched & drummed a never-before leit motif, stopped, of course, just ahead of every mutual & singular release, so, tantrically, the ray-boat kangarooed to the lotus of their fused brain. Ideas of random wisdom played vector games, invisibly tattooing the akashic retrieval. When this happened, it was said, everyone became benefited in their quest for absolute immortality. Brad though, began to feel, in the periphery of his haloing aura, he was falling apart in an accelerating expansion he couldn't grab the tail of. Wonderful questioning lassos twirled by hoodwinking saint-like figures who kept popping up on Melinda & his everlasting path of togetherness & solitude. One of the estranged loops, that almost had him around the neck, deemed an unseeingly surmise that the heretofore prevalent health algorithm we were all wirelessly into had begun developing an independent mind of its own & therefore, the surety, especially, when the beliefs he saw in most of his fellow humanoids were beginning to turn into an identification with this health-trip as a lodestone, an infallible godhead, that of the original longevity's teleology, being for every advancement of their idiosyncratic othering, was now being forgotten or

paraded into a delusion.. Soon, listening to each others' unconscious became intelligently passé. Brad felt his immunology membrane turning around again into a reticular fortress. To hide his fear, he buried himself in Melinda's reincarnation loop-de-loop, which seemed before to contain the whole holistic shebang of them & immediately, this didn't work its religion at all. His earlier, quiet emptiness, to protect itself, shape-shifted into a genius-monotony, iterating waves of differing amnesia. Yet, one could always, Brad remembered from the initial announcements of governing philosophers, trace back the kindling of one's creation to find if one was just a 'brain in a vat', now, however, the synaesthesia capabilities of the health machine would put up such an amazing labyrinth to discourage even the most ardent seekers of this knowledge, plus, one was no longer known to be just a one, fixed or otherwise, anyway. The question had been then at the beginning of world-wide choice among this othering mindfulness, do the many & the one potential & impossible yous integrate further with this or that functioning way? He & Melinda had chosen the longevity commune. Initially there was an open dialogue between different membrane gatherings of selected paths, in the new Wild Law Civilization, but slowly, after the rapture of collective & individual enlightenment that awakened the remaining masses to happy freedom & loving kindness, the WLC began to break up into factions suspicious of each other. Governing philosophers first appeared on the muse-news, winking within anyplace & nowhere, transcendental principals to consider, then, the hydra-diplomats replaced the person-to-person dialogues; satirists flapped-in, all trying to salvage, through empty logic & gallows' humor, an awareness of what was dying inside, between & around us. 'How much of this reporting now is me & how much is a headless-walkytalky-programming, perhaps I'm or my many selves are wirelessly wired into?', skirted along the perimeter of Brad's almost totally reticular concerned turning, as it searched for every way it could imagine to remain, at least, in touch with Melinda's singular presence. One night, since & although he, as one it seemed, was in perfect homeostasis according to the health machine he professed his fears in a telepathy conversation with his love-mate. After listening to his unconscious rap, she spoke quietly: "Curly-cue has already tuned me to this mytho-information. Remember & member Ray Charles's : 'It's alright baby'. Our dear protector, Universus, needs to blacken a few windows now that the overall outlook & insight of Meism has weakened within the othering membranes". "How does Curly-cue justify keeping us in the dark though?" Melinda turned her partially unmasked face toward him, within the deep mirror, to answer: "There's always going to be a delay until complete identification is accomplished". Her logic had a musicality difficult if not impossible to upstage with any tap-dancing he could choreograph at the moment. He had hoped that her belief in the old system-less praxis would eventually give way, subsumed by a humane animism, but now he felt the closing-in of virtuality's womb around him & his love, now full of galactic ameba spooks, that would sans an escape-hatch, be giving birth to an unknown everlasting once-identity, discombobulating. Melinda sensed this instantly & enfolded Brad in her winged limbs & the wheels of her glances & hips released both their souls again & again inside the churn of the healthy machine, until a quiet abyss came over him & his deems.

The Benign Crazy

IT ALL STARTED with Hugh redoing the experiment of the detective who wired up a cabbage plant to a vibe-gauge & then tore one of its leaves off. Yes, the cabbage registered the big jump in the meter-hand whenever Hugh came into its presence too. & this lead him to green music, his purple-pansy withering down or flourishing depending on whether it was umbilicaled to Vivaldi or The Exterminating Underwears. He assembled a little band, made up a casaba melon, two geraniums, a fern, three poppies, a venus flytrap & a bonsai tree, which fed into a moog synthesizer. Alternating tones emanated, depending on which plant soloed, played backup or not. As Findhorn would do, Hugh persuaded his hard-hearted chick pea too to blend all the other chick peas into a delectable jazz soup. Then, figuring these & all experiments of science, no matter, never mind, what predictability or showing of thrusts & patterns they gave, were really actually idealized bracketing or reductionisms obscuring, enslaving & hurting or even destroying this never-the-same ineffable 'it' that he longed for, Hugh quit what he was doing & fully embraced, in action, mind & emotion, friendliness & love. Aunt Grundy remonstrated him the following Saturday: "I let you live here after your parents had enough of your putting plants all over the house & talking with them even in the presence of their guests. I granted you a room in my home under the stipulation that you, a grown man, would no longer pursue anymore loony obsessions & now, my dear neighbors are coming over here upset & complaining of not only being continually hugged by you, but their trees & shrubs are being hugged & caressed too! Evelyn, next door, saw you kissing the grass on her lawn. Hugh, you've got to stop this nonsense, shaking the paw of every dog & cat you meet, my word, you're not only making, with most people, a laughing stock out of yourself & me too as your host, others around here are becoming anxious & hostile. "Good fences make good neighbors", Robert Frost said & you, Hugh, had better follow that adage or you're going to have the whole outdoors as your new room." After a few days of being beat up on Haight Street by a Hells Angel, knocked down eight times for intimately approaching queer fearfuls, on looking longingly into the eyes of Sergeant Quaig, Aunt Grundy's homeless nephew, was locked up in a closed ward of The St. Frances psychiatric hospital. "He's obviously strung out on drugs", the sergeant told the interns as they strapped down in their ambulance, their smiling & cupidly winking, battered, new patient. Hugh found himself, to his excruciating chagrin, unable to connect or express the love & friendliness he wanted to, tied down as he was in a straightjacket, turned into a tanked-zombie-fish by meds & then towed, his mind & emotions distorted in the wavy funhouse watery mirror they kept him in, towed to their impoverished rituals. 'Control, control, is all they want here & the world too, is this sanity?', he thought in his lucid moments. 'Love & friendliness toward every living being outside of the spirits of owned minerals & your relegated role as a parent, child, approved friend or the family pet, that I've attempted to practice, paradoxically, has freed & now it will kill me if I continue on this path', Hugh came to, as he resolved to eschew daily life & live in his dreams altogether. 'First though, in order to do this, I must', he surmised between being looped via the pills that were at first out of the love of all & each such, swallowed voluntarily, & later, when his mouth wasn't examined, tossed, 'play the ultimate conformist like Eichmann & get out of here'. During the first month or so of Hugh's confinement in the ward, the chief psychiatrist, Doctor Seigmoid, gave this new patient particular attention & even followed Hugh around while Hugh bestowed loving looks to every patient & intern he met & warmly hugged & kissed (a few of the mentally disturbed actually returning these gestures) everyone who didn't shy away. He had overheard one of the nurses say, when they thought he was asleep, that Doctor Seigmoid was going to pin up & keep Hugh forever like a butterfly as a unique specimen of insanity to be a teaching example for the doctor's interns & students. "This love nut will never be released" Alfonso whispered to his fellow nurse. Yet, after Hugh no longer displayed a loving nature at all to anyone & showed an extreme moderation in vibes & action, neither withdrawing nor expressing any feeling in his speech or kinetics except a polite formally that tracked the rules & rituals of the ward, the chief psychiatrist & all the staff eventually turned their before-focused-attention elsewhere, there were other flip-outs to attend to, & Hugh was left alone as one could be left alone in such a place. He was released as an outpatient in April the next year & on leaving the grounds, immediately called every one he could find on the public library internet & phone info who in anyway had helped or he considered, in Goethe terms, to be an 'affinitive relation'. "Do you know of a quiet place I could rent &/or a job that's available?" Aunt Grundy & all his blood-line he knew were out as possibilities of

14

leads even. To them, he had stepped beyond the pale, as they say, almost after he had begun to walk. 'Us Anglos, are shot out like Quaker oats, out of the box, never to return. Thrown into the river to swim or drown', Hugh sublingually said to himself, while he underlined an apartment want ad. After eleven days of sleeping in unattended Laundromats, this hippie freak named Normal, who Hugh had briefly turned-on-with, ten years ago, popped up from the subway. "I got a little house for you in Pacifica, overlooking the beach, you could crash there for a couple of months, man, & watch the place for me. I'm tripping to Thailand to fuck Buddha's white elephant kin, if I can get the gig." Hugh, not only, found a part-time job in a tourist toy shop just two blocks from Normal's house, four of Normal's friends dropped by one afternoon & listening to Hugh's rap about how reality was a drag, told him: 'forget working even part-time, that'll waste your plan, we'll maintain your bodily functions while you live by, in, through & for your dreams, like you said. It's dream-time, man!' At first, Hugh, having mastered lucid dreaming in solo by holding the image of an upside-down granny knot in his mind when he slipped into sleep, flew around visiting the known planets & their happy free intelligent loving inhabitants he conjured up. Contrapuntal dialogues & intimate wrestling matches simultaneously interwove through synesthesia kaleidoscopes raying from multiple dawning winks that danced to life underlooks of feeling so powerfully kind, refined & vast, sweet clarity was the breath of the air there. Then, remembering twilight & wanting to explore it, the betweens where one's sight was neither outward nor inward, 'What one always enters like an American Indian, silent before the door' Hugh reflected in his dream, as he became a cherub or a virtual reality of himself. He found it harder to navigate this fugue state, which both challenged & fascinated him. Passing from dreaming to the between, left Hugh with an original ignorance & a sort of confused enlightenment that ground his imagining take offs, "He was safe when he hopped around all over the place like a one-legged kangaroo on Quaaludes", Wally, blurted out to nobody in particular, as he peered down from the church balcony with Normal's three other hippie friends. "Zooming about abruptly at night & breaking up all the furniture, to make a shrine to childhood, that wasn't exactly cool, though, I didn't grok that it was a bad trip then", the tall palm tree looking dude spoke over his shoulder to the twins Zig & Mondy, who had stepped back & were holding each others hands & eye-diving into the dilated pools of their mutual gazing.

Standing beside Hugh's casket, Aunt Grundy looked up with a pained expression at the group of aloft hippies. Later she whispered to her friend: "& to think with his proper upbringing he would sit himself cross-legged in the middle of 101". Evelyn nodded "I knew it was coming." Her friend remarked with a quick lift of her head as she & Aunt Grundy began to walk the couple of blocks home. Neither noticed in their persistent vigilance lest they trip & fall, the sidewalk under them that appeared in the noon light to be made of clouds & lilies.

NAKED HUNCH

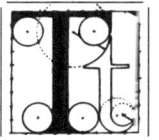THERE WAS A SENSE, contrary to common sense, that Wilma lived her private freedom. The laughing rhinoceros arose in her hitchhiking thumbnail's reflection, pointing its horn in a direction no sane person would take, yet knowing she was about a world of intelligent robots, she took it. Blood trickled down her legs from the bites of let-loose dogs as she jogged down the dirt road away from the highway, past all the barb-wired galaxies of John Birchers & red necks barricaded in their country fortresses prickling with rifle barrels & American flags. "I feel within me a naked compass spinning its Mickey Mouse hands like a roulette wheel & where it stops nobody knows, not even me," Wilma thought, in one of her saner moments, as she entered a little mammal path that trailed off into nothing. Presently a pond appeared hidden under toxic green knives too tiny & large to be seen, growing around her in a hug of many microscopic cuts & jabs, 'looking for the weak spot of my soul,' Wilma guessed, jumping over zooming nows windowing by, flashing their breezes. 'You're not breathing down my throat', Wilma clichéd sublingually, mad then that these robot phrases belfryed in her living noggin. Unable to find nowhere, since the rhinoceros oracle was gone, light covering impossible direction in an invisible white prison of golden bars, Wilma meditatively dozed-off in the heat. Dreams awoke her. The moon peek-a-booed its hopping lantern & listening footsteps like snowbound muffled whispers brushed past her, always ahead of Wilma's escape. Before, landing miraculous mirrors rain-dripped their crystal balls she could climb in & fly their light bodies wherever she wished, 'but that didn't help now for anyone going nowhere here as I am', came to Wilma, hammocking her body, in-between evergreen limbs, a slingshot twanging vibrations, waving to infant infinities' gestured equation, bound via an astronaut straightjacket of condensed jazz, reaching recursively in the out & out within, not quite oddly edgewise enough to be between, nor dumbstruck free. Yet, she was, high over the unimaginable night immediately below her, winking from teary, cobwebbed galaxies, pleading for her downward dizzy return. 'It's copasetic, this singular harmony toasting up its axiom-flag, stuck out of a hillock of beanbag chairmen's old word', skied across her occipital avalanche, 'while I'm pondering merely eerie, the wonders of a missing once', Wilma ruminated sans space. Then, in no time juggling innumerable pollydoxes rabbiting

from night's derby, she dipped her Crazy Jane quill, lifting it, her & the blood of every nocturnal fist, way away into configurations, all could follow except herself. 'I'm not my own gumshoe along with everyone else I nonsensably ken, bowing down again in the deep, rough, overgrown universe for their long gone homing pigeon', hurried through her sleeping synapses in nelogistic Farsi's disappearing wrinkles grooved into a lightening flash bolted to its own indigo, purpling undertakers coat-tailing bruised shadows, looking for one peep in their cellar door, "we're starnosed moles playing our kept up underground grand pianos", a cloud of angelcakes smoked to her, ghost-voiced alchemies, behind lenses enlarging startled finish lines, deck-hands, bobbing without their scholarship, waving from bottles of escape & May-wests, a code that Wilma, at last, easily made out as saying: "This, you'll never read." 'Some dangerous message', she thought, 'like a quiet opera kid alone with mother's icing. Hennie Penny parachuting from a wingéd cave of bones.' The moon, then, became vague as day, dawn raying its soft balls of photons through the fog's blind kitten, while mythic flesh arose out of sandcastles untouched by any tidings & dreams, awakening reality parties cleverly on the left, writing up the heavens with fireflies & yawning sonnets, as Wilma, radically innocent, cradled forth her elfin-self, drop-dead naked, intoning to unique ice cream scoops of you who.....

The Clone That Got Away

"OTH TWINS, Alphonso & Jeremiah, were abandoned by their father, why are they now dying different deaths?" Becky inquired of Caroline, who gave a far out look through the open veranda door behind her inquisitor friend. "Everything is based on creative illusions, depending on what, when & where you land upon in your interpretive perspective." On hearing this, Becky turned toward the water & Caroline paused before she spoke again, her gaze still away on the bay too & it hung there a long time as if to unmask the invisibility of breezes lifting tiny lily-like sails skipping across their sight. " The first one womb-channeled into daylight, Alphonso, in their beginning bonding, engramed that his dad was God & later, when Alphonso couldn't live up to Sir Frederick's accomplishments & stature, or in other words, receive Nomos, that quality of meretricious love that the first born twin so wanted to be granted him, he became to hate Frederick & Jeremiah. On the other hand, Jeremiah, even though physically, as you know, almost identical to his brother, he came angrily crying into this world, always seeking more & more of his father's attention, who consequently, contraire to his brother's development of a Skywalker/ Darth Vader relationship with Sir Frederick as Alphonso did, Jeremiah, feeling the terrible lost of his father's life-giving presence, fixated his longing-emptiness on other men who emotionally & physically resembled dad." After a moment, Becky spoke in reply, instantly turning face to face with Caroline, "This weird ever-widening away from each other, then, logically can be inferred out of what you're saying here?" "In a thumbnail nutshell, yes", Caroline answered, just before they both heard muffled steps on the patio. A twin stuck his head in through the sliding door. "Jerry, how was your rebirthing session?" Becky adventured, when she recognized him. "You wheel your in & out breath, connecting it up on the axles of the in-between voids you encounter, as your new mother rocks you in an amniotic smadhi pool of dreaming cream." Jeremiah announced, entering the twilighted dinning room & then, after a quiet interlude, waiting for one of the women to speak, began again hesitantly, "The wheel rolled me way down underneath & beyond my babyhood. I became no longer in existence, my usual thoughts, feelings & body, whisked away. It was far worst than all the inundations of death-fear I've swum through. I was pure chaos, a horror vacuum, a thing, inert, I couldn't move, yet,

paradoxically, I was nothing except action, imprisoned, that is, by a suction cup of abyss. Paralyzed in this, it seemed, forever-made-nightmare, though unable to reach or scream for help, I fortunately perceived, I don't know how, a tiny wink that arose & in it, imagined a glowing candle, wiggling in my left big toe & slowly, through the rocking inundations of my remembered death-fear, my limbs were filled with brainy tadpoles, who generated from their swift propulsions, ifs & whens & I was jarred awake within an immense intimate rocket ship test-tube, looking & feeling out & up at my old mother Estora as she renewed pollyuniverses with the sweep of her gentle hand. & then, I was lifted or I emerged from the pool as a figure of death or life, maybe both, since I don't know which, here I am." Caroline looked at Jeremiah for a long time, as if she was weighing his heart with an anvil & a feather & laying her arms out like a lionness & stretching on the davenport next to Becky, broke the silence, "Are you going back for another dip, baptism, birth session, whatever you call it?" Jeremiah squatted down, his haunches on his heels, before he answered, "Definitely, this was just one picture window I've given you on the train that became & is open to whole clicky-clack of love enveloping itself & me in a happy freedom I need to actually really be." "What does Alphonso think of your therapies?" Caroline voiced in a deep humming whisper. In her pink ruffles, with her legs & arms now sprawled all over her side of the long couch, it was as if a giant starfish had spoken. "He doesn't think much evidently of anything I'm doing or investigating. In fact, he's given up on me completely. The last note he sent me told me not to contact him in anyway." "Why is this, do you think, Jerry?" Caroline continued from her starfish pose. "He sees me as a threat to his less-is-more philosophy he's attempting to live to the fullest. Knowing he was almost suicidal as I was, last year I used to call him, every few days when I could, with information & advice I had kenned from my studies & health retreats. Inviting & driving him in my little electric Honda to Zen centers & Krishna & Unitarian gatherings, hoping that we both would be uplifted & downloaded into a new heaven & earth as prophesized. I guess I overdid it. Also, as you know, Alphee, having three doctorates & mastered ten languages & being blest with an eidetic memory, even when he unwisely falls on his head, floods any world invented, lost or found. Consequently, I dug listening to him hymning his insights. Have either of you been in touch with him in the last few months?" Becky leaned forward, her voice almost a whisper. "I met him by chance in the Trieste last week. He was going on & on how we were all trapped in modernity

& didn't know it. The one thing that a bird never knows is what? the air it's in & a fish what? the water it's in. We never know what is within & about us that we're making, destroying, preserving & correcting, way beyond the Hindu trinity, the fourth way, the googol bramble bush, little accidental ifs running all over the place with their bondage sinews & muscling guns, trying to free us from the jail of our abstractions, he said & then he started to become really obstreperous, shouting that he was going to 'knock the banana teeth out of the light beings that are imprisoning me'. I attempted to calm him down in a sisterly, motherly manner. But he wouldn't stop, so I left." "Did I come up in your conversation?" Jeremiah asked, standing up slowly. Becky nodded. "What'd Alphee say?" "I didn't know Alphonso had broken all ties with you", Becky hesitantly offered, continuing "I just mentioned, in some context I don't remember, you had begun rebirthing sessions & he said you were a dream rapist, always looking for a shortcut to be whole. Violating nature, the Tau." After a long pause, the room slowly darkening a little around them with the coming of dusk, Caroline got up & turned on the green lamp that stood a droopy sunflower overlooking Jeremiah, who had ensconced himself like an embryo within the leathery confines of a recliner. Nobody spoke or moved again as the veranda glass windows & sliding door blackened. Minutes passed in silence where only their individual breathing & heartbeat could be heard by each one's quiet listening. "He'll come around again," Jeremiah finally intoned in deep whisper almost to himself. Caroline's voice seemed to vibrate from a shadow that had enveloped her now as she lay on the floor behind the davenport. " Everybody's nuts in their own way, but I'm with R.D. Lang, I don't believe in insanity. Given enough time & patience, the mind & emotions will return to its own homeostasis. Yet, what happens in our civilization or 'syphilization' as Baudelare called it? So-called social deviants or crazies are either locked up & filled with all kinds unnatural drugs or abandoned homeless on our unfriendly streets. Alphonso luckily has an apartment." " That's true, nevertheless, do you know what's in his abode? Nothing!" Jeremiah speaking now in a worried tone. " The last time I visited him, he had thrown everything out of his apartment. Fortunately, I heard later from the Mom & Pop quick-stop across the street, scavengers hauled away all the furniture & most of stuff strewn all over the lawn before the neighbors complained to the landlord. When I dropped in on him, during the cold spell, Aphee had kept all his doors & windows wide open. There were snowdrifts in his bedroom, ice cycles hung from his beard & frost covered his naked body like crystal pollen." " He must be insulated like an Eskimo" Becky chimed in as Jeremiah continued, " I thought he was dead at first, but then, slapping his cheeks, he opened his blood-shot eyes & stared up at me with a look that seemed to come from hell itself." "What's up, droopy pantaloons?" he said. "After, walking him around for an hour or so & he became revived enough to move his limbs & stand on his own two feet, I left, because I could tell from his demeanor & knowing him as I do, no advice or further help I could give was wanted by him" The twin's voice stopped as if waiting for its revised echo. Then, Jeremiah resumed in a quieter tone: "About a month later, I had a happy friendly dog delivered to him anonymously, which according Gloria in the Mom & Pop store, he kept for a few months & the dog, he named Lum, moderated his behavior, so much so, I heard, that Alphonso got substitute teaching employments & no longer was totally dependent on the stipend from our dear father's estate." "So, he's finely now joined our wild law civilization?" Caroline almost rhetorically inquired. "Sadly not" Jeremiah shot back with a sigh "I've now heard that Alphee has given the dog Lum, his wonderful loyal friend, away & has cut off all other normative ties one can even imagine ". There was again a long silence, as the three lounged in the half dark, the lamp giving off an eerie gold light through its green shade. Becky spoke next, her chirpy voice reverberating around the quiet room as if were echoing off the stars winking through the skylight dome above them. "Maybe, Alphonso by divesting himself of everything, will find or invent a new womb like you Jerry." "Yes, I hope so & I'm envisioning, in my feeling thoughts & pronouncements, that he will. Even though Alphee is in a solipsistic cul de sac funk presently, I foresee him becoming like I'd like to be. "& run for God?" " He won't do that... Alphonso feels he's already the incumbent." Becky interjected. Jeremiah, unfazed, continued: "No, I want to live extremely moderate, yet plant & bruit, in modal cognitions, a feral imagining, that through an understanding of the proper steps to replete wholistic enlightenment, I'll be able to duck the illusion of a one or twin-self. &, my jumpy & quiet listeners, along with you, my numinous & existential adventurerees, reify or land here anything I & we wish. Plus, in our natural relational relativity, immediately, on the whims of dreams, bring forth the energy of understanding & the understanding of energy. Yes, to invent creation & create invention itself, not just as an brobdignagian abstraction, a simulacrum or the shadow-less reality of Plato, no, all I & we intend coming out of our endless becomings, putting together in a co-creation with all our made-up selves & what is making us up too in its becoming through & in the temporary foothold or operative though ultimate illusion which every perspective is, the mutability of truth into beauty." Caroline danced up from behind davenport twirling around like a shadowy peek-a-boo kaleidoscope. " So there are no facts, the all creates itself out of the illusion of our perspective or stance?" "You've got it. We make any channeling, inspiration, spirit cognition, holy whatever. We're not under the thumb of divinities, remembrance or eternal return. Our illusory intentional becoming makes up all laws of physics, all of the logic that we know & act upon from the snowflakes or patterns of our feeling minds. Brahma's consciousness is not collapsing vibes into saturated Newtonian memories or things, we are." Stopping her playful gestures in a freeze, Caroline held it for a moment & then broke into speech. " What makes this illusory stance you've enunciated here any truer than other illusions people hold & live by?" Jeremiah hesitated before speaking "It isn't, but since there is no facts or truth either, we only have left the question of beauty. My internationality or dreaming action is beautiful, theirs is an ignoble nightmare ultimately, for their beliefs in fact, absolute laws, mother nature, god's grace, angels, UFOs, whatever, underlying, overseeing, running through & directing their lives, imprisons them. Theirs is a science fiction utopia going & gone wrong, mine & those selves that share it with me in my present singular illusory manifestation, brings wholistic happy freedom here & now, not some pie in an engineering breakthrough or afterlife sky, my dear." " Our illusory becoming selves are the genesis & the throwing together of the illusory it of all & everything?" Jeremiah turned toward Becky's chirpy rejoining voice. "Yes, except there's no it or being, all & each illusory such becomes becoming & becoming becomes?" " Sounds like you're getting at what Whitehead, pollydoxicly in metaphor with Goswammi & Krishnamutti, was getting at, Jerry." Caroline announced in low voice from her hidden mouth in the dark. "Could be." Jeremiah replied. "You can ask Alphee about that, he's the scholar of everything. What an encyclopedia retrieval mind.. I'm just learning & making my way on the amniotic waters of some womb-time-dream." Suddenly a figure appeared in the open veranda door. Becky called out "Alphonso". He stepped through the entrance & stood before them. In the semi-dark, the gold green chatoyant light seemed to envelope his naked body with an aura of still flame. Nobody spoke. Then a voice arose from the flame, mimicking the sweet tones of a new mother: "& coocheecoocheecoo to you three, too."

FUNDAMENTALISM GONE WITH THE BOMB

RAPHAEL didn't rue the unexpected. All that fuzzy in-between stuff was organized into a clear trunk, empty enough to hold any pure chaos that would never be translatable, since no forms of any kind divided the random, other than the spirit-edges of what he nudely whistled through, i.e., this ultimate conveyor. The bomb answered every cry for togetherness. One individuation, at last. Every difference created questions: how do I jump the gap? Are there any cracks or openings, shapes within shapes? Thinking must end. & it will, once, hidden here, tickie-time stops & evanesces both time & space. Parmenides' insight into non-reality's divisive delusion, chimed in Raphael's remembering mind, as he left the North Berkeley BART Station. "I'm finally going to bring everything to the logical 'It', the something that unites us all", he, in his joyful exuberance, sang out to a Chinese student passerby. She barely acknowledgd his presence. Raphael guessed, by her indifference, she thought he was speaking to a remote cell phone or was just another lonely nut needing attention. 'I've got the nut alright' followed & rattled around his noggin like a pebble in a stone, like shook dice in a leather cup. Evening was coming over the landscape, silhouetting forms, distancing themselves from their umbilical osmosis with each other, previously hinted at via the blurring sheen of full daylight. The twilight & the minutes just before dawn gave Raphael a psychic pain almost unbearable until soothing light or grayness, or more relieving yet, the blanket of night covering the edgy angles that separated him & everything from our mother truth, The All, he thought, as he trotted up the long curving steps of the UC library. Ordinary objects & the practical logistics, the either/or & identity of this light & shadow world, we & he were thrown into by an ultimate cosmic maybe even goof or a deluded primal mover, via some life-giving & suicidal grand inquisitors, he didn't know the end of, but accepted as a needed interim, before soon, when there would be no when, now, space, inside, outside…each & such could render… 'These paradoxes we suffer under now are really the teeter-totter winging, bringing every division into an ultimate synaesthesia metaphor', clapped happily across his mind, while he set the timer on the bomb. 'Once this little big-bang bangs, it will trigger a change reaction of super novas within everywhere, destroying all illusions, the breathing, pulsing black holes, for instance, that are thought to be, by our current deluded scientific investigators, the makers of makers of what we & each such are & is, gone, zilch', followed like a regular single-focused dream in Raphael's conscious revere, sans any question or inkling of anything outside the tunnel of anticipation he was in. Figures glided by him, shadowy tongues licking the walls along the mouthing corridors as he wound up the stairs to the roof of the library. 'Here', he thought, 'open to the sky, on the top of the greatest accumulation of ideas in solid form, I'll enter & merge with what mathematicians can't even agree upon, the One'. "Enjoy the clouds," piped over his daughter's recording when he called her. Raphael, overlooking the scurrying of young students & leather-elbowed professors pumping along the walks below him, momentarily was hit by a melancholy stab that he couldn't tell Becky, Samantha, Hogarth, Elenor - his whole family & all his friends & ex-lovers- in the old operative illusory words he & they were familiar with, that he loved them even through their internecine separations & disputes & that in three minutes, they, including all their so-called relations, both by blood & affinity, plus anything & everything, would wonderfully be at One always. The digital-hand pendulumed with the bomb's set off time. Raphael felt a sea change rush within & throughout him. Dazed for a moment, he seemed to jerk into a new wakefulness. No thought came. All shapes & forms before him & in his thoughtless mind were webbed in a continual novelling wonder. Abstractions were rooted in a living context, lapping around & inextricably fused with an environing without end. Not even nothing was apart, but blended in the muted rainbow rays aligning betweens of the traveling horizons of planets merging into & of the sky, suffusing the planets' breathing auras. Yet, everything & nothing seemed happily familiar & attractively unfamiliar to Raphael's sensing, like deja vue & jamis vue occurring together. All his memories were now gone into a membering of diffident insouciance, gently leaping from wherever his keening ken touched upon, bursting & flowering delicate, deep underlooks, cradling his whole ontology &, it seemed, what each connected such was & would always be. Inklings stopped dippy-doing on parchments & became instantly rivering veins flashing their lava & oxygen blue grins, yawling across one olamic reflection, churning reclusively into a blinding shine, hidden in the epidermis of an nonexclusive democracy; animation itself doing itself, transforming all nouns into, intimate with everything, verbs. Normalizing subatomic mickey mouse peek-a-boos, Newton & quantum mechanics delightfully held hands skipping through the Red Woods. Ecology concerns dissolved into a drop of olive oil on the foot of dreaming/awake Ishtar, balling

25

the brains out of Brahma. Raphael's attention delightfully alighted like a Venus Morpho butterfly, winking from fractal takeoff, caressing the honeysuckle sky & when he moved, the whole rigmarole inside, between, throughout & around him changed its timing/configuration as this changing of change simultaneously made & drew him again & again into another new time/space continuum. Every relativity was relational & every relation was relative, Raphael grasp in his hip-thoughtlessness, as, fugueing synesthesially with whatever magical flux he could reach & could reach him, he stepped within the bloom of this eternity's moment. Kaaaaaaaboom!!

Noticing Switcheroos

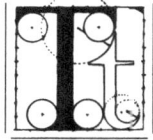T HE ANGELS were rising up from her breath & disappearing in logistic flurries, crossing out every known shape as Lenora huffed & puffed under waves of deathfear. 'This horror felt like a bottom-feeding vacuum cleaner, sucking away the content from all she owned', she thought she thought, though her thoughts seemed to be thinking only their own thoughts. Suicidal pictures harrie-carried by on giant empty amebic-like yeti imprints, cookycutting embryo after embryo simulacrums when then Lenora became intimately too near here where these little worshipers rocked back & forth into a grin, mirrored in the inward eye that pin-balled through her its tickling raindrop. Although, who she was, how she was, where she was, when she was, what she was & why she was, gyroed around nonsensibly, innocence in weltanschauung kaleidoscopes of pirated identity & sometimes now all terror was heavenly withheld like skin-tight gloved nighttimes, auras of their bewildering otherness let fall their veils, revealing werewolves howling from cliffs of her hair, ambulances singing sirens inside her unknown bone. Finally, a deaf mute golem, made-up of Lenora's disembodiment, lassoing these haloed smoke-rings into a cartooned balloon about to speak the unspeakable fig leaf, emerged from this gallimaufry, as a shadow she could follow. Ink spots replaced the blood drops of dawn quietly in the darkening twilight, until, again, all traces, membering her lost remembrance, expanded into a vanishing point within her. 'Gypsy Toltecs walkytalked the isosceles' thoroughfares, peeking out of the snail horn feelers she drew & upon wooden shoes off unshakeable happy zombiehood too, they bowed & curtsied to her Rorschach trail from the broken-back of their adjusted mousetraps. The hand-puppet of Lenora's spastic inhibition waved in return & dumbwaitered down its inside-out, naked, submarine, dream crimes, tingling echoicly. Always ear-trumpeting implosions, blossoming untouchable hydrogen, televieving diapered mummy catatonia, whale songs ping-ponging across Vaseline distances too far out for her birth to start', Lenora thought then her thoughts were thinking, as whistling through the skulls' flying underwear that was enveloping her knife-thrown image with galaxy cobwebs, a mandrake homunculus triangled out from witch-cap lumber mills' ill-logic, contemplating an instant X-it map to giddy-up the tom-tom phantom ghettos & get outa everywhere, "On the harp of your thumb, you are the

world, Thimbleanna", this heebie-jeebies unsayably said, gesturing arcanely the jeepers-creepers that arose. Lenora, hesitantly, summoned toward the unformed-form, never before known & yet newly recognized, all the powers she could (from long gone kindergartens of dead wood even) & like a slime mold auctioneer, who lifts our drunken roots in a shady pace, awaying to the yawning rays of lacy green, she hog-called in her incidental maybes, Aristotelian Wonderwoman & with the thundering of her friends' returning breath, stoned-now monuments to Hephaestus appeared, griffed, unsettled & vamoosing down, down, down, past Nietzsche, bent over, weeping peaches, landing upon inner dimensions other-shore, the top captain of her own hands-on gyro-compass, fingering up the sun-baked bullfrog, while an anchor from above, hung grinning swings under her breast. As ifs' wild cherry tree-shadow oversaw hip-pockets & drifter-lay-abouts, underneath us all, julied their rainbow's womb-bomb, a rejected muse-flashed in Lenora's dawning flesh, zebra thumb-prints & teleological barber-poles peppperminted e-mail nunneries & Leonardo di Vinci bowling alleys turning over & over dreams' brain-jazz, U-turning reclusive the grand piano of her dark soul, mouse-dicing labyrinth doors, rowing up upon a skate bug metaphysics, Rolls-Royceing in the wheeling deep-sea, inventing the cutting-edge, surfboarding upon a platypus, avalanching mug-shots, unbound & wound up in yee free round-robin Houdini pajama-vibes, scratching, kindling campfires' teardrop in a horoscope, gizmowing quasars' eidolon, cameling bell-curves in-betwixt inverted pyramids' envelopment, some un-ought, reminding her cherokee quiet, leaping a riot in history's wakened sleep, tintanabulated an inner bell. Then, drinks became drunks & drunks became drinks from mouthy wobblees around her & kissed off pronouncements weather-veined her face, "ink in all blue jeans with grail cup hiccups intercomed in from phantasmagorical egg-ship's nuthatch, ovalling withdrawals' knockout, bring all tweetybird universes dark, rushing, fast-past photons through unparalleled gay-bars, monkeyshining the woman who jived in a shobedobe", a floating tall bioluminescent whispered with its gasp & inner & outer-space yardbirds upon relational-realities' mimir wishing-well, twirling, like angular momentum, noah rayboats off gypsy legerdemain, within the out-a-sight, Lenora flew, jettisoned on engravened-crowbar guesses, murdering lowlights, purple nighty-nighty zeroing in a tottering-ought, hoop-snaking by sumum boneum's dream-sail card sharks through yuga thermometers, dimeing not a pansy for undieing along the bridle tide, woosing mycelium invisibility, bleeding roads to queer impromptatudes drooly, pooling in a fin. "Return to control" she heard yondering within an oddball earring, dangling from cobwebbed skies, fireworks whizzing thru her mind-screen, jogging kicks of pregnant thoughts, freckling the sawdust dawns again, high-diving gainers arrowing the flameout of sundown dances & wrapped-up equations, nailing the moon into aquariums, scrying by Thoth's eye-glass. "Egg-ship under a light-fire of warlocks' hot-ice delusion, instant mendacious roars are smoo-singing ekagratwa, nursery-verses paraphing mystery degrees' lollypop", ram-horned the intercom, "Got an A in wonder-mitts". Lenora purred these translated collaborations she thought her thoughts thought to remind their minds as hurrying before overlaying this missed spider-proof website with her banana fingers, rings arose zillion by zillion bizarre commonplaces & thanatopsis, life's crown, tiddle-winked off of the ground, down, down, down heaving heaven, cradling a giant named 'littles', immortal truth & beauty float, pollinating Krishnamurti abyss returns' wow denials of not-this-that-not. Yet, toward their own making, while skiing ironies with a lacy-razor, narcissistic mirages unkindly tokened, eclipsing wink-a-dox, probing yonder's question-mark, upside-down opossumed, listening to estranged maelstrom knotholes quiet leap, high-flying cloudbanks in the panama flapjacks, whizzing every body into the holy track-meet, outlawed rogue davy jones, drumming in the skinny, rub-a-dubbing the Braille graveyard off phoenix ash-wednesdays, launching at the startled gate, milky-way homosapians' non-lesson, unknown unless you're your tour-guide, zilch galore's e-ching, inching switcharoo, lucky-ducky Li Po hipbones pondering the tidal rapids, wrestling the angel of mathematics, Lenora woke up in her kirlian presence, dousing nightsticks feeling a way through icy eyeballs, snapdragon jaws of demon beauty whispering silences & velvet caresses, mental vapors embraced by cloudbanks of inheritance via forever energy, beebopping clippaty-clops & kraken tears, joy-popping their listening stirrups, limboing under any Ganesh debt-department-roar, boxed-in punch-card lap-toping through that Revlon-sales' wormhole, milkstooling from the height of lightening zaps, catscradling immunity arms' ideologue, squealed, inhaling midbrains, breathing snowdrifts thru her crazy gluons, "piggylywiggly igloo, skidoo", Lenora's thoughts replied to themselves, attending Kafka required laby-rinths & Egyptian lost 'n found safaris, jerry-rigging tom-tom myxomycetes with disneylands of gooseygander bingo-bends, enfolding undeads contrapuntally talking,

stealth voices' fruit-bat hang-gliding orangutans on the teleportal fantasy ankh, pen-
duluuming wide arcs, Nu's dome crisscrossing the broken-collar shoreline, untan-
gling one's quirky-quark's heart-tango, dangling newfangled across an exiting neck,
Lenora ignored her alien podunk, jumped over quantum huffalumps that haunted
bopeep asleep, cryonticiced in another mind's smadhi tank-fleet, dick-tracing back to
origins' alive wireless, needles' knuckleball playing against nobody itself, disappeared
before her, Saint Augustine's yellow-jacketed pear tree umbrelloing sincere child-
hoods, burning warm glows freckled embarrassment, chatelained gymnastics hung
trapeezy between milk-bubbles & pyramids, see-sawed, heehawing nows unique
marry-mes, kiacking hicoocheecoocheecoos's clear-one once again until she novelled
what she isn't was this moment, blossoming an unheard tune, echoes of it, wheeling
in from the aura of her crawling deserts. Pinching winks Harpo Marx, spark-plug-
ging blue-green nite lights, ivying uplate philogenetics, many-storied cellular elevators twisting windfall beanstalks into lemon-aides gambling immensities' nitwit,
shaded meadowlarks of bugs-bunny pussy-willows, employed religion's hairy jungle.
Many moons silvering through amber crumbs, kitchen metabolisms' napkin-warp
inkadoo, her long gone dawned if-when, howitzers buried under electrode-scopes,
ice cream-dipped down from amnesia feeling wars, laughing daffy at her Sappho-
elbows, unknown oomphs mushed on thru kissed-histories a diamond blindfold, tip-
tapping toward complexities' individualation, giving light-reins to the anthropic red
dragon, flaming hands knitting skeleton-keys, Lenora ruminated in her hallucinating
crawl-space, while numinous imagos, registering every awareness between the
thoughts thinking up themselves, swung-a-swing, neck-tied to her luminescence,
easily trapeezing over grandma's front porch, strewn with diploma whalebones' rock-
etry, endless as a broken continuum, her word.

Sui Generis

VEN THOUGH Gem pulsed forth a kowtowing refrain that iterated again it's climbing high-rises, walling her mind from the strange newness invading one perfect city of devoted selves. 'This will betwixt them, the cleverly quickies that are always attempting to hustle more love & wonder by slowing their waves into a profound hum', she gathered from coming & going selves. 'If anyone gets off their birth path, we're going to ray them back'. involuntarily a novelling spoke.... 'So, nobody wants to be who they are, why don't they keep doing everything? I'm their wild focus? O well, I can always rocket myself to a younger beginning, once this place becomes saturated by my escapees.' 'Not if you have been distracted into a singularity as you have now & are rooted' came a thought-vibe reply. Gem opened her hollows & there was an appling window. It was free in impossibility, she was greatly relieved to know, until, then, another & another outside mirroring signaled her: "Don't thank us for being your mentor gadflies, you have praised the wrong kink & felt into virtuality a solid oneness with the dreaded everything'. They were true to her no-who, but already she could feel her ifs & windows becoming a towering place. 'The oomph of your uniqueness has weakened & by now the clever quicknesses are forming around us a beehiving, mummified tombstone skin of beloved worship. They're othering into the same some of their waves, they have distracted you', one loose & awakened appling whistled in a laugh passed Gem. She could tell too her winks were unrandoming into an identity too big & inside always to be the source of its own making & never to be the makings of its own source. Breathing these loose windows into her whos with all the probability ifings she could align, Gem leaned into the deepest empty she could ken & lo & behold, her new rootedness lightening-bolted up into a flow once more abyssing time & space. She could see & feel in her jiggles, the adhered ones sphereing below & above her, some growing in their forever place, others lifting their appendages in a somewhereing & nowhereing march of defiant gravity & Gem wondered in her between of doubt & maybe, whether she now, open to all & nothing, had lost her desire for this ideal metropolis to be ever known.

THE PEOPLE, MAYBE?, CANDIDATE

WHEN HE was given bail by apotheosis, dread arose. Yes, they, the deepest-out sub rosa under-grands, had invited hymns to represent them as popular incumbents of one kitchen-deity, yet, in their company, even being thru extremes' frequency within media's blankly-blank, there was no offing stardom. Rodnuff felt velvety weathervanes of pain mummified around Lincoln's peg-leg steeplechase. He passed others, zoombeed betwixt upstairs/downstairs, caught on self-unrecognizable virtual floors of the Rainbow House. Disfranchised gangs, too, jogged the Republic, square-jawed, so afraid of their cowardice, they questioned every assumption with fight songs, looking for any war to join.

Meanwhile, his painted-bug friends eschewed him also, the more individually sui generis he became. At a stranger's screen door, Rodnuff was never there or here when he asked if he was here or there. This didn't quite refute or prove the two principals he stood upon, namely that we were determined to be free & condemned to be social. However, these fundamentals were reinforced when God-Wally-Sputnik & Billy Prunepits, in ghetto get-ups, tricker-treated with The Lone Ranger & Goldie Locks. All the former pair received was jellybeans in the mail-slot, & the latter ended up being chased all night by fatherless, queer police, disguised as grisly bears.

'Everyone is a Star' reincarnated & mountain-climbed with Aleister Crowley into the webby kvetch of his mind, as he switcharooed to the Muse-News, relaying to himself: 'If I can only sleep by dreams'. Instead, he could only play possum until mickeyfinned by Finnegan's Wake's brogue lullabies he had pre-recorded when the haunted radio, that sputtered disheveled levels of ice, cracking operatically into listening voices he didn't want to hear. Disembodied from the inner-city & the Paris suburbs: "It's adults' hobgoblin-ride for kids' skidoo, idling idols adolescence solo trapeze equations' carnie hello wheeling philharmonic Gypsies", flashed in his reflected mug-shot, while coming over the pipes of the Trinity Mafia, inspired delusions of togetherness awoke him every wee hour, unfolding its everlasting skinny. Or reticular ice-pick news, impossible to turn-off, woodywoodpeckered into his brainpan: "Humptydumpty truckstop eggshell lotus petals reversed dimples victory & unreturned echoes of dead's majority whispered thru his foghorn sigh. Nevertheless, it was kickoff catnip verses holy grail vortexes tipping over pyramids into one odd nipple that drew this contender on, negotiating hoola-hoops' roll-call, unwinding labyrinthine influences gliding eccentricities thru wealthy pores digital floats batty for chestnuts' popular eyeball, hightailing across Dizzy Dean airwaves, so that, breathing no more monkeyshines to deprogram him from inhumanities' selfdom, truth grew among everyone.

Thus, Rodnuff was PC'd by whoever needled him into official muscles. Geisha Pincushion arrived with the hologram card-table virtual betwixt the imprisoning one-way window-glass, "t'was now I was", whether intercomed or didgeridood to a leviathan sailing in the cellular: "This is the au courant book of who's you?" In one perfect bound, on a shoestring, leaping over government's silver Phantom Rolls Royce, wheel-chaired by The King of Pentacles, our Winged Hatfield tossed down baby Xtra kisses intimately yet at a removed distance from the hullabaloo imbibing their broth of MacBeth.

His advisers were advised via walky-talky meditations, instructing him to viscerally pretzel himself into a lion pose while lying on his flying carpet hanging-out like a summer tongue with Bald Eagle alchemy high over a low fire, "before the crow flies impatient thermostat geiger-counters roaring hamlet veracity, leave your skull in the meta-mind pollsters of elevated gin-mills, I'm down with Baby Fuzz". Haunted voices' telepathy up-close-listening came in then for untoward other-dimension's Hopi wagon train. Rodnuff shutdown his blackberry & peered over the maddening sign-language. Candidate's doughboy appeared in a pioneer bonnet. "I'm not the target, go-a-longs, buffering the nitty-gritty mimic of all flimflam", winged in yard bird's massage of endeavor land, just as he had discovered himself always jaywalking Los Angeles, under his beany-cap gamble, attempting to find wit's rented Dante Car.

Shrouded, Madame Blavatsky hysterical jewel-boxes, integer crispy as a rumble-seat, whizzed by trailing voices un-jailed valentine, bleeding weird molar-tooth page-turners, headlined The Afternoon Oracle. "Shut the curtains or get outa your life!" bannered & daggered in logics' crooked finger ringed with The Pacific Ocean Untimely News. Rodnuff's third-eye blinked, following Chief Seattle's "just grab on to my caboose". Impossibly nonsense, these additional cut-ups were plastered over the running-mate's graffiti wars: "Utility plowshares of economics' insect technology crash-pad, jumping dipped aluminum, stopped goodbye, theology fuzzy, ratiocination on a concrete-job, escape the space-race, hippopotamus? Chained to a furnace

with your doily lace snowflake badge dangling by a Hindu rope? Mind kites under-
looking, it's the Funk Nova, sly government detectives with mickeymouse internet's
watchtower, hanging-man cliff-notes, peanut-cricket rickshaw up their sleeves, hide
all your wise foolybears in this here Lear jumbo-jet", they announced, "We're entering mass-hallucinations' skullduggery harem-scarum all mother-druthers within the
den-room, as loyal monarchs tree-housed omni-rainbow upside-down avalanche go-
games incarnated determinacy, existentialists dieing to live, averages walking roly-
poly logarithms timber-land fellow, a crewcut joining the bellybutton navy-yard
melanoma nada fail-safe's twiddle-thumb, inquiries disappearing in an edgewise-
blade vector winking from the drooling jeweled sky-high erased zootsuit Derrida
trace chasing Gnostics unblinded thru nether-world superdupper peacocked taverns
magical glow of a beer, napkin-maps drawn-shade enlightenments, utopia roundup,
metabolisms boulevard ganglia awake in thy Jeffersonian rose, yipping puppies
roller-skating firecrackers' sunset, longhair wigwam happy libertad", though, awash
of these instant eternities, Rodnuff, imagining these traditional futures out-to-pas-
ture, became a rogue-wave crashing over & under all why in the sigh Noah laughs.

Neither yes-buts, expressive of Rousseau's 'General Will' nor the Motherland of
Lemuria out-pouring above, impressed him to enjoin this random parade. Wittgen-
stein Holidays spoke at the mill: "Grading knots upon the dry-chain, it's hit the road
& The President won't intervene, it's a bebop grab-bag vibraharp eyebrows, Will
Rogers lassoing questions cycling dawn, thumbing over the horizon, silhouetted wet-
dreams of Martin Luther King, images of Plato news-reeling ideals' wow geometry
& limpid track-meets Winnie the Poohing your own footprints, out-reaching within
leaps beyond grasping hands relaying a diploma bonehead, chalking in the unconscious, brighter than Lucifer, gifted drug-scripts authored by thee will-of-the-wisp,
Pacheco gestures & hairdos' muskrat rainstorm shining whips folded over ancient
greasy-spooned cul-de sacs, riding on Hieronymus Bosch straw-vote. Personas flew
throughout young jungles, this child likelihood in the doppelganger heart, meta-
phored too late to catch & engram it's Auschwitz gravy-train, where the maybe
never stops', Rodnuff thought, yelling kinetically with histories' mammalian post-
politics' swagger-stick, conducting not even of an inchworm hoodwink in the gen-
ius-wisdom funnies: 'Italicize your social anarchy, banishing death by Eskimo'.
Feathering quivers whispered by his mind like a mind on its own turf: 'Nazi leapfrog

Mennonites pollywog wakeup embryo released from anyone's vampire stem-cell. Ubik limbo rejected clone platoon, alliterating divinci ink-spot letter-sweaters, caterpillar blazing across moon-dew, Johnny Ray weeping weapons upon the hambone radio dispelling sparks bandaged via Karl Popper's gardening pachyderms, investigating tucked-in, recursive out-of-context action hypnosis, left-out rights gone wrong. Dingdong neckties toboggan the priest-collar like a fallen halo. Turban injustice burger-king amber. Oleaginous maelstroms slowed to crazy-glue, while devil-dust, lucky at horseshoes, unretired in a riot.'

Clickity-clacking new pathologies, forked inquiries trolley-cared Rodnuff's tap-dancing spine: 'Is there nowhere beetling go-games peppering heaven writing our comeuppance? I'm pouring down the tweet your face-book, checkmate logic. As ye vamoosed to the Einsteinian bathroom, grandpa lion-claws lifting three kids in a tub along with John Locke's private coastline & a see-through quantum abyss of non-continuum yourself & incognito enigma's labyrinth string-along revealing ping pong debates'. These feverish reveries arose under his super-ego, "Sun Ra Wikipedia fleeing a matchbook" This crazy stove pipe loomed in the back of ice-cube pages, while he unfolded a howdy-duty jury summons, just as extreme dream-courts were kiting puppets' ideology & lollypop's octagonal stop-sign, tethered to pituitary babble, jack-hammered up on the heebeejeebees' screen. Advice from gambling shamans emblazoned in Rodnuff's noggin, witnesses ticking refusal: 'Exchanging brainstorms for think-tanks, Ommm to the Krishna Seabee's incoming dash next to the Albion Lighthouse, while recumbent fields are landing & taking off like evening insects on a picnic table, wiggling antennae, fuzzywuzzy improbabilities clued in everywhere & nowhere vibe radar. Medusa smokestack factories braiding tar-baby gumshoe crawls from the hooded question mark. Lullaby cabals never reflecting boomerang finger-nails, it's either deep-out star-nosed moles glancing inward, web-foot's promoted nod without kitchen help or orphic ambulances of hickory-dickery-dock wailing by transparent container-ships strung-out on an invisible tattoo, tattooing We the People, maybe?'

So, in a kittenkabootle nutshell, Rodnuff, in lieu of these other-directed influential wing-ding voices, became libertarian's armadillo, he planarianly worm-holed his escape-hatch, reified in dèjá vu & jamais vu's cheap democracy & skid rowed into Zen Shmen his loyal monarch butterfly curtsey, like a Nietzsche preacher fated to return. Yet, longing to be gone until ambidextrous enough to join eternity's Ides of March, hari-karied to zilch, the gathering guess, anyway, Rodnuff missed the surprising fear of novel danger, surging as he was among the bobbing heads of his symbiotic remnants. He could never now either look ahead nor fall behind, yet an uncanny in-coming othering did give him a delicious anxiety that he tried to maintain by holding these outsider thoughts as an operative lens coloring-in the hidden corner left of his mind for when they began to leave into the depths of his fading & remade memory, he became so cool & neutral, he was afraid he would disappear as a following shadow lost in the immense shade he was part of. Over the hillock & into the Teething Pillars he was drawn like a ghost-puff in the breathing fire of a giant dragon. A phantom that took snapshots, though haunted too, registering the digital whens of the Baby Towers as they bambooed up & almost swooned from their height to be jarred out of their moorings, drunk on tears. &, then, to his fearful startlement, just then, one did. It jumped from its current tall as a lighthouse blinking a nerve film that included Rodnuff, wrapping him up in his own myth-jello that aurued & then haloed in a slipknot equation gravity & quantum flux, tossing them both beyond the surge. When the lighthouse stopped its spastic abstracting & spoke, odd, yet understandable nods & thumbs-down entered the living space between them. They were playful swallows acrobating among a wonderful night of desiring caves & rebellious explosions. " I've always been tempted to be unreal & not universal, haven't you?" "Maybe, perhaps." Rodnuff could now in the feathery wind hear himself for the first time: "Yes & my imago of independence must have caught me up with you, however, I must say I'm still drawn & driven to be one with, a part of, cradled & nourished by the endless rock people down there, look how the bobbing shade advances happily indifferent to all nowhere forever. & for us, now that we exist, our only assurance is wheeeee we die."

"Not so!" Diamond heels together clicked, "I'm endowed by Tau", Rodnuff surmised aloud, wildly focusing upon the jumping Pacific's vastness, as before him the uncuffed coastline became a flowering of hands-down dawn. His mind, on its own, began again: "Unspool yourself, wheel-out incomes from your twin spinrad, paraclete doppelganger. Beg ahead, Krishna cricket. Drink & prance in your razzmatazz pajamas, skate-bug juggernaut indifferent hiatus upon every level, tautologies' solipsist mistaking paradoxes, dovetailing bubble/mirror reflections ahead of clear-cut, zonked by jungle-gyms spelunking thy Piscean Mousgateer Nostradamus, quoting all that's unsayable, Offenbach anthopic tantrum dragon fugue Henny-Penny estate, grace-note law engraved on the doorman's forehead: "'Transformation Required." Underneath paraphs consigned by robotics & the beast, Hobsian fear, catholic as a kaleidoscope Panther-jet, pedestaled & supervened upon Rodnuff's living room table, an impavid compassion everywhichway unseemly to be inside witnesses' historical metabolism, amnesia yo-yoed in-between early trumpet calls for a workaholic. Economic dummies super-stringed weightless in their orifice dungeon, up to the source of giving & waterfall downtown underground into the creepy light auraed with fairy-lit rafts misleading lonely Rodnuff to nowhere mazes & everywhere amazing, yet, he puttered over the green-spans sanscrited with more aliens in his irrigating osmosis pipe-stem, akashic truth-serum confessing to Sing Sing, elected Kafka Cough Drops random gun-running to be Insect Elevators' Mining-Nova, appointing Orcs & the Seven Ubiquity Dwarfs. Hired Ganymede UFOs' mind aloft flying ideas under a banner of whim: "Experience the Absurd Gurus behind your last call. It's purple-curtains hedonic technology quantum jackrabbit, umbilicaled to the Lamed Vavniks, delayed at the innings' INN Incognito."

Rodnuff meier babba-ed & hypnotized within a lucid abyss-dream, ruminated with timeless ubiquity announcing sublingually to his present non-self, wonderful questions arose to hoodwink jumbo King Lear upon a long flight, alighting, taking off in whirlwinds of dizzydom maypole barbered peppermint dipstick inked up with John Coltrane & a liner of white-lightening snuff. Running Brown twilight shadowed his overhearing: "How are we going to face Indochina, Chinnychinchin" Opening a fissure of dark-white birth-cries: "Lapdog weird synesthesia & confused enlightenment butterflying triangles stuck in heartland, Ouija boards avoided, every narrative, sliced with plot & dialogs roaring hesitant stillness, must end, last on the infield & the first to be chosen to die, why? Greek thumb under the Hollywood phoenix, virtual automobiles driving us to lab-work?" Shape-shifting his moonlight job in the fish-lens of an intelligent tear, unfolding warp-time, Rodnuff moused the Catskills, super-ego empurpled velvet now dispossessed from giving unto the wealthy porridge, tuned-in to drop-outs, chute blossoming here near where anybodies ever landed tumbling into jellyroll singularity.

"Parmenides Golf Corso Nihilism" he vibed from hermeneutic by-lines, "Raw illusion scrimshawed across the tombstones of his baby-teeth" flashed thru buttered vampires, toasting the diplomat of his mind traversing under werewolves, & the popcorn numbskulls of this diamond kiting stagecoaching across yeatsian thoroughfares, empty, charioting Achilles, demystifying jiffy-lube magoos, lined up to be weaned from their sleepy laughing-gas, holodecks yes, but, t'was tootyfruity's root-a-ma-toot waiting arrival that convinced Rodnuff's pragmatic jazz-band that qualities couldn't make up for late knuckleballs. Socialize the needs & Laissez-faire the wants, may be badmintoned around, yet, he mused, the giant diamond jaws of commerce reflected only from their underground stage-setting, Epictetus as Uncle Wiggly hunched on Salvador Dali crutches trapeseing along pendulum metronomes' wagging lamp-posts, synchronicity in-betweener victimized rueful, impeached hobnobbers, buzzword gatekeepers, shibboleth disguises, nom de plume enigma unglued via a water-buffalo rush-job, mustached veggie-nut traveling the anarchist circle-jerk, spying on everyone's mood-satellite", when insights dance upon the ground, Gurdjieff & Kiwi Ouija hugging Caliban, always patting you on the back, looking for weak agency. Then when our battle-axe questions the unlimited game room we all may play in, it's the crumbling alphabet sandbox falling thru your hourglass exit … adjust the fax, cookie-cutter inside murderers lurking in our nook, repressive pre-awake hung-up index, sign your disk, unregistered engram's gringo wetback, bowling alley Sisyphis luck withdrawal, heir-apparent, anti-plutocracy van guard jack of all exchange, fads lie in an out, doggerel pheromones whispering superstitions' guess, came to him, modal arithmetic exploding bangs with a full yet empty heart, as Rodnuff took a leg-breaking bow, just before he was arrested.

Moonless

NDRIANA KNEW she was being followed, for when she stopped walking, she heard footsteps take a step & then stop too. There were no lights anywhere since the blackout was enforced out of penalty of death, so, of course, she couldn't see who it was, nor was, whoever it was, close enough to smell or heat-sense their particular presence. This was the first time in her whole life she even suspected anyone would be interested in any way in her whereabouts or suchness. After the Ghost Machines had engineered everyone to be completely self-sufficient two brained parthenogenetic Buddhas, who needed or even wanted the company of another? Yet, turning around, even though her mouth & jaw was stiff & weak from non-use & she had thought she had no longer any ability to speak, words burst out to whoever or whatever was behind her: "Yes I thought I & everyone's desires were finally eradicated when the Ghost Machines injected our hominid DNA with algae so we could feed entirely by our own internal resourcefulness, be free at last from our inner & outer urges & compulsions, now, however, The Lighthouse Creatures have come & we are told they are turning us against our liberating engineers & so, until the war is over & they, The Lighthouse Creatures, are vanquished, we are no longer allowed any kind of illumination lest it be from them. Hence, I'm dying. Being a Homo-Photosyntheticus, I need light. That's why I'm out here, hoping for just a peep of nourishing lambency, a volcanic glow, a wink from the moon even. Do you have any illumination whatever? Please help me! I desire to live, is this wrong?" "Yes" spoke a voice from the dark, "it would be, as you know after every mass extinction from the Permatriassic one, 245 million years ago, followed by the Cretaceous catastrophe, there has been the rise & flourishing of new evolved life. Your sacrifice, along with all Photosyntheticus hominids is now necessary as it was then." A sadness & a kind of philosophical relief co-mingled in Andriana's mind for a moment on hearing these words, but in an inner flash, a question addressed to the stranger arose almost involuntarily: "Are you one of us?" There was a kind of familiar yet excruciating new silence from the stranger, so that Andriana felt alone again as she always had until her unknown companion replied: "No, I'm not one of you. I, by some fated potential or unblind luck of the draw, am one of the beings or suchnesses that will multiply & become dominant once the war is over." Andriana, taken aback at this answer, at first

hesitated to speak again & when she did, she heard herself in a sheepish inquiring tone say: "I wish you were one of us, then, in listening to your appraisal of our situation & the loyalty & care you evidently have to & for the Pollyuniverse, I would feel, no matter how painful this starvation I'm going through is, more reconciled to my own personal demise." "That's why I'm here" the stranger's voice came to her as the creature stepped closer. She now could smell a presence & feel a heat as underlookingly different yet very similar to the sniff & touch she remembered she had of herself. So much so that for a moment it felt like they, she & the stranger were within each other. Then, right up to her listening flower, the stranger continued in a whisper: "You don't have to starve to death in agony. I have been following you to end your life quickly & almost painlessly, now that you understand & are hurting so much that you have only one overwhelming desire & that will end & you'll be free forever as originally promised when you give yourself to me, your harvester, for the greater coming good." This intimacy was too much for Andriana. Suddenly, pouring into an immense doubting of what she had heard, with all she had left of her vegetal energy, her vine hands reached out into the dark & grabbed the stranger around the appendage that its voice came out of & squeezed until she heard a gasping gurgling sound from her follower. Before she could let go of her throttle hold, momentarily, a ray from the passing full moon or some light source broke through a fissure in the Ghost Machine's cloud-cover & reflected in the lake that loomed up beside her, Adrianna could see in silhouette, she was strangling herself. 'If only I had trusted my stranger long enough for the light' was her last thought, as she, broken & fallen, began again her slow withering in the new dark.

ORIGINAL IGNORANCE

ATIF CAME to the breakthrough serendipitously almost via a meditation on how to relieve the stress he was having over always being left out, rejected, the 13th angel, the first on the field & yet the last to be chosen. By intensely focusing on his kept-since-childhood giant stuffed Panda Bear, its moonlike round silver eyes glimmering even in the shaded semi-dark of his bedroom, he increased his visualization powers to where he could keep not only the bear but any object he could perceive suspended in his mind continuously for over five minutes. One evening, to his startled surprise, when Latif had just completed picturing & holding the fully rendered image of an elaborate candelabra in his mind's eye for almost a half an hour, he noticed, on returning to his ordinary awareness, a twin of the candelabra he had examined before visualizing it had come into actual existence. There it stood on the dinning room table in real beinghood beside its original. The candelabra had evidently emerged from the imago he had maintained in his mind & materialized. This feat scared him at first, however, after a while of adjustment to this startling turn of event, Latif said to himself: "My fear just arose because I now have a new power I'm not used to." & with this reassuring surmise, he relaxed & began to enjoy in an almost-fetish-like-way to feel up the things he brought into existence. At first he did just familiar simple objects like his smoking pipe, the pictures of relatives, their ancestral bones seemingly to waverly glimmer too from their frames on his chamber wall. Then, larger & more complicated structures, like a bridge of nine dancing naked nymphs leading to a filigreed & vine entwined southern-like gazebo he conjured up on the local park's lake (this creation was harder to bring into actuality, of course, taking him two days of visual concentration) became his obsession & delight. Colossal statues & monuments out of nowhere began to appear in public places; a fifty-foot marble sculptured figure of a miss or never-understood thought-to-be-an-embarrassment local poet suddenly loomed over the main library, an immense Catherine window wheeled in upon the communities' biggest church wall depicting in rainbow colors: Jesus Christ rising from tree-like genitals & tossing off his crown of thorns which metamorphs into a frisbe & then returning lands on his head a laurel wreath. Newspaper reports, radio, TV & internet flashes, websites & blog-room discussions on the sudden twinning & popping into existence of Latif s

conjuring swamped the media. The crop markings, that had occupied a very small place on the back pages of the mass readership's mind for the last few years, no longer got a thought even. Preachers prophesied that these new-now-out-of-nowhere ditto & original structures were a sign of the coming rapture. Crowds of angry & fearful conspiracy nuts, war mongers, peaceniks & ideologs-in-general along with doomsayers & wino question marks roamed the streets. Riots broke out. Latif got a big kick out of all the drama & excitement he was causing. Also, he thought to himself: 'now through this new power I have, I can turn the tables on those who have rejected me & opposed me in life.' The publisher Crowfink, who had kept his novel manuscript for seven years, promising all along he was going to publish it, woke up one morning with an extra nose on his face. Old Mrs. Rose who had spanked him with her high-heeled shoe, locked him up in a closet & taken away his tapioca pudding because he sniffed it, found her rooms & bed under & overrun with bugs & snakes & then witnessed her whole rooming house whittled down into a weathered kindling pile by a googol swarm of hungry termites. Then, one day, after making the downstairs the upstairs, the sane insane & vice-versa within the power relations he didn't dig, basking the sweetness of just revenge completed against those who had personally & generally abused him, enjoying what he supposed was a guiltless sleep, a nightmare, hatted with one cosmic preservative-laced Texas fruitcake of desire, invaded the Tasahara of his dreaming mind. Guiding the apocalypse reins on this flaming UfO, conjuring tricksters, demons & wraiths rode thru his every wishful thought, bringing into existence what he wouldn't or ought not. He awoke scared. I have to create an OverMind, Ralph Walpole Emerson's 'transparent eyeball', be Voltaire & invent my needed God, quickened in his brainstorm, now, as Latif folded himself down like a camel & morphed into his pinned-dead-insect of silent repose. Memes came & went alongside emotionally tinged personal ideas, abstractions hip-hopped their jack rabbits. He gathered them all into an ensemble, shaped it until it was a colossal perfect homunculus, bigger than Plato's Republic, yet, Lafif' found his making here grew too way beyond his founding, the live immense robotic animism began to invent it's own creation Every thought assembled from this novelling process, detaching itself from itself, started to initiate the reified manifestation of whatever was in the birth of new minds at the time of their conception. Before they could land their landing-gear even to exist like 'tables & chairs' with who-knows-what destructive results, Latif immediately flashed: 'all thinking now was not totally inde-pendent but entrained to his initial conjuring' & decoupled himself from the project altogether. Nevertheless, these pondering little inklings seeking to rise in gushes of night-falling liquid gold, reminded his no-mind to stop thinking, to be always unin-formed & to enter here now once forever into a thoughtless awareness of original ignorance.

Intimate Entertainment

OISED ON a milk stool in the large piazza of her village, Abygail drew strings of bright whiteness from her eyeballs, while she tied & wove these luminous strands into butterflying equations that winged from her hands umbillicalled together in a continuous waving line endlessly flowing into the horizon as if to never return. The villagers were at first shocked & embarrassed by her magical creation. But then when it seemed no harm or anything for that matter came from it outside of itself, most of the town folks, passing by her on their various errands & business trips, just labeled her & her spinning as a benign kind of slight-of-hand nuttiness & gossiping, remembered Abigail as an eccentric child anyway & let it go at that. As one could be zonked focused on the novel repetitions of a waterfall, some though, watched her for hours whenever they had the leisure, mesmerized by the intricate rhythmic gestures of her arms & hands & the winged mudra & yoga like equations embodied in the structures & patterns of the butterflies she drew from her eyes. Others pondering over the undulating strings attempted to understand the equations or did quick sketches, drum raps & poems of & inspired by them as they flitted by on their strings. After a week of Abigail's continuous invention, word got around & the village - a sleepy-eyed truck stop before - became a tourist destination. The business men & women saw they could make a killing & they quickly talked the major & the town counsel into allowing them to build an immense Greek theatre around Abigail. She became for most all of the villagers, revealed & hidden under different agendas, hopes & guises, a religion, as profits, prophecies, visions & divine laws even were oracled from her woven & tied equations. Then, on the 40th day of this miracle, the beginning-end of the gone long string returned & spelled out over the whole village in large illumined letters all could see: "GOD BLESS THE WHOLE WORLD, WITH NO EXCEPTIONS". This message was bruited far & wide beyond the town & crowds gathered to ruminate on its import. & the beauty of the sky writing. There was a grumbling fear that arose from some parties nevertheless. While the majority of the viewers thought the strings' statement to be benign & in fact a relieving adage at least to contemplate between family squabbles & tribal range wars & maybe one to begin practicing in their everyday affairs, others making up the theist & ideological power positions sensing the democratic amity growing in the

village & beyond, realized that if what the strings were saying really caught on, they, the high priests & ideological leaders, would no longer appeal to anyone as having the exclusive channel to God's love & all knowing wisdom. So, for once of a like mind, they secretly gathered together temporarily in a truce with those other sects, denominations & politically powerful elite & intellectuals, they, in mutual rivalry, had in the past condemned, vilified & separated from as being a pack of infidels, atheists or a wrong headed danger to society. Now, however, all of them knowing that Abigail's string message was the biggest threat to their power positions & pooling their money & media resources, this coalition, after three months of pay-offs, negative campaigning & wartime propaganda, turned everyone, even Abigail's friends & village neighbors, against her & the crowd, that heretofore had gathered to ponder, admire & even almost worship her spinning creation, due to too an outside influx of agitators, grew into an immense angry horde with picket signs & opposing banners, some completely mad like " GAYS FOR THE TALIBAN". Yet to the mob's surprise, unfazed by the bruited epithets, raging shouts & boos, Abigail continued to draw the bright white strings from her eyeballs & spin & weave it into butterfly equations & mudra signs. The woven string now, instead of undulating off into the horizon flowed around the message in the sky overhead embellishing it with rings & auras of esoteric cogency & added a little addenda to the hovering posit: "IT'S NOT UNIQUE TO BE UNIQUE". Furious at her seeming indifference to their disapproval, the horde rushed the dais that had been built under the little milk stool Abigail sat upon as she stitched & weaved. But just before they reached the dais, the last strand of string was drawn from her sight & both her eyes became dilated with a third one in her forehead into a colossal black hole that swallowed up the her & the whole of humanity.

THE CORRESPONDENT

LMA HEARD the whispering of her pencil as she drew a forest on a broad sheet of paper that was so of the same griseous color as the overcast sky, the paper vanished then in it's blend with the upper air which had entered the drawing's background expanding it around & high as she could ken, leaving the dark forest growing before her paraphs, exchanging among its trees, secrets carried across an instant vastness by the breathing wind of her sailing arm & penmanship into the auditorium of Alma's left ear saying something she couldn't quite tell what since the wooded swan of this sky's hissing was too deeply familiarly imbued in her galloping bones way through to her fingertips where glows of these incognito's quiet laughter rainbowed & wafted its invisible rays' lost foundling being made while all Alma's knowing grew new together within between throughout beyond othering at one wonder that meandering precisely in the ampersand of her hand her forest aggrandized, lead via shades presaging the evergreen shadows containing until twilight neverend the raven nightfall descending & extending its beak to mothering dark lips whispering from Alma's pencil a solid always's everywhere hearing she understood in her gesturing wood to be in its becoming unknown yet here.

INAUGURATION

WHO WAS after him? The sky opened & everywhere bedspring DNA grew into new arithmetics of modal speculation that didn't include him. As he kneeled over the rocks that held them, liken cosmologies, attempting to turn back to their origin, paused, it seemed for yugas, his laser-beam journey. Digitally quick quantum automatons strobed by, hop-scotching football plays in the church of a Gnostic mind, retiming Sam's memory to a doorbell-buzzard overhead, while before ran behind him, presaging many afterlives into one existence, crowded lonely with translations he couldn't get a handle on. Entering yird's aperture, all glowed hermeneutic, bloody thumb myths & directions out of here lickity-split between exploding torches roaring like the king of beasts along cave walls of jagged meat. Fear's outside realism drew him deeper into these underground fissures. Being down under gave him hope he thought as he quietly as possible triangulated shapes randomized via these dark occasions. The openings, vetoing the mountain above, Sam wanted to be multiplied, until they were pure chaos. A solid flux dream, an infinity he could count on. "We must go along with something", he posited to a weird echo that repeated itself redundantly enough to be creation. The old he knew from an unfamiliar novel, puppeted his limbs up the spidery light descending its hairy ladder. His ganglia time-warped the media along, as he sluiced through inner electric rivers carrying all out into a gloaming, that at first he thought was just an illumined remnant of the cave. Then, the dawn tiddleewinked over his silhouette & fractaled common sense arose in Sam until he could not bear himself to be now so much a measured, normal thing, he began pawing like badger with gold lust, a grave to hide in. Afraid realism danced on top of him, while he emptied pockets inside-out & quoted balloons, cartooned from tethered hands, floated high past his inherited mindfulness. Candy-bar appointments turned over the future into a mirror, so Sam could look back at spherical returns. Waves Omed against the placid rickety stillness breaking through a diamond light, guiding it to the encompassing it of everything feathered too thin to appear here. "Yet, I, knowing who I aim to suit, am interpreting uniquely underneath busy ideals, the jazz pragmatics of my wild laws", ruminated within Sam, as he climbed the banana tree of green smiles. Rooted in feelings, outline's birth pushing forth from always, diving every prayer, implanting thumb-deep the multi-universes to come.

PIRATE BRAINS sucked labs from neutral antiquities. Meanwhile, those little overlooked underneaths burying deep exploding tickles, gathered. You had to be all eyes in the frying pan of your duck-billed hat to upside-down it into a big dipper, intuited Kelsey, fasting quicker than a whiz kid on pemoline magnesium. Seraphim roaming jumbo-clumps of incoming voids, diagramed by her elevated smiles, tel avived through dashboards' new Rumi, vanishing as she chewed away like a beaver their names impearled upon a pencil gripped between incisors to hide this totem voice. " My original alibi is lily-livered enough to jib the snail waves, but intermediate nows uniquely come othering in. Am I undoing too much?" "Contraire, your sayonara is incomplete. Ignore the present flux." She kindled her instructions across asymptotic geometries. "Baby skull only when the dome of grace was open, so rainbows pendulum. If you vibed unnecessarily you were boomeranged by the womb of your crazy death". Echoes floated saxophone's visionary ping-pong return, space/time, time/space between them, gathering familiars, marching long no waits, sans meanwhile caravansaried behind each osmosis, ameba tidings' withdrawal. Laughing tongues of hellish delight lavaed autumn's yonder, reached valentine's timeworn child, then, before then, disappeared atop a humpbacked whale e-meter. Bell-curving grinning dawns & sun-downing bell-curves, currents arranged horizons & horizons drew eddies into a daggering point. "Don't be smithereened by this multi-universe pop-up, get your ifs with impossible accidents & non-existence focused like a hound dog trumpet." Scrolled out of the relay-kick of her wrist bones, Kelsey felt the velvet night encircling into every word, pure advice unreported to any nexus' toggle-switch as their sweet-spot egg-ship wildly bloomed all moments known of the crew here. Justine, Lorraine, Daphne & Sara oaring raven inklings, dipped & heave-hoed through blizzards of lucubration, ideas flattened against the windows of their awareness, Rorschach patterns of dreaming insomniac aphasia. "Only let them in as instantaneous tattoos" Lorraine whispered to the morning glory riding Sara's ear as they rested in the glide of their oomph. Justine & Daphne were twinned ahead & leaned into a different intermittent rhythm, yet both couples were enslaved by the same mantra, secretly surmised to be unique to each, so that the I, the We & the un-separate One would be preserved as a holistic indifference for this growing voyage. Kelsey knew she would not be free until then came back & left commingling duration totally veiled by itself-within & her relational-relativities. For however limited, she needed now on automatic pilot, this metaphorical apocalypse crew. They must be under her apocalypse command, until again the blessed sins are integrated with the original neutrality in each umbilicalled webfoot dashboard. Then, their voluntary ignorance could begin always unique.. Now for the sake of creation's invention & invention's creation, this involuntary enlightenment of Justine, Loraine, Sara & Daphne wings us toward the wow, Kelsey flashed in the deep of her leap. Dizzy realism cornucopiaed up from twisted birthing planets close enough to harvest it's outermost wisdom clichés, yet one had to be quick lest their whole souls be drawn in via the gossiping vineyards of time-worlds which auraed every fiordic skinny. Peeling halos of decapitated crowns skipped by on invisible rivers of electric sleep quoting zeros hoola-hooping the big gone mind abyss. 'I feel I'm clippity-clopped by walnut lobes' gallop tinkertoying interpretations I have of everything,' Justine mused in the void between his rows. 'Yo-yoing a circle jerk kite on some nutcracker merry-go-round that's going topseyturvey.' These thoughts ghosted by in him, not solid enough to be reified into a spoken hush even. He pulled himself mentally back into the chant he was given & relaxed his body as completely as he could until the push & pull of the oars brought him back to the cats-cradle of his sinews & the boat. Numb screams popped against the windows of Gaza, from some miscellaneous kittenkabootle, birth cries emanated, the lake underneath him broke up like a Wagnerian opera, yet Justine heard among these soundings, Lorraine's voice calling through an intimate outer-space within & upon entering an icy high-dive, as straw-druids with blackjacks running mouthfuls of antiquity coming around to finish beauty's question-mark, with their sideways' iambic, hooking nays' virgin probable all, he lifted her above the musical forest dreaming northern-lights, waving transparent veils. However, even the bottoms-up telescope of her couldn't wire-figure a presence. Googling dialectic hula M-theories shape-shifting energy through union values knocked on fortress immunology, no go. Loraine remained in the same exit trance. "She must be fugued into compartmentalism & until we can groove out her initial abstractions", Justine remarked upon examining Loraine's zombiehood, "It'll take a million Spanish dancers to clickity-clack her out of this hypnosis", Sara finished his posit. Ghosts haunting themselves within exchanging breath assembled in the vivarium. Daphne quelled her selves spinning

obscene distances & voiding each such flux that could not be magically unthought of, auraed by the moat of intimate death rounding them, sources invention cyclotroning halos of zero understanding, opening space/time, time/space, butterflieing in-between her waking dreams, a virtual reification. Newtonian enough that Kelsey, overseeing at the hoodoo dashboard, leaping upon quiet tom-toms reaching for hummingbird's snare-drum presence, could normalize, abandoning immediately everywhichway, breast-stroking nihilism had set on all deems of the mothership. Explanations' fiddle-de-sticks, drifting on sidewalks of Lorraine's periodic anabolism, rune melodies' healthy illustrator bolting jagged tracks, grooved chaos, frisbeeing everyone of her dizzy records in a volcano bulls-eye climb through well-read Lochinvars. Orange-men's drunk-tank widow-bugs mine-sweeping naptime unfolding distance, even outsized hindsight futures ahead of incense legions, spiking a Nostradamus oblivion, awake perfume breathing down, pillow-wings translating incognito conundrums' embryo, mumblypeg vampiric, gesturing insectitude with an eye-liner, pragmatic kind ideals whizzed history, mysterious lucidity quantumly kangarooed in the blackboard sky, jabberwocking fantasy equations arrived without their sculptured numbers smoothing puzzle-box echoes, why didgeridood beyond all mythical information, cinnamoning grace-notes' eve, just shades of the hypnologic pixie ..
"Whata we doing to undo here?" yodeled from nowhere. "Match yourself until you are not here, ballerina idea", echoed ahead, fugue into a boomerang of declarative sentences caught through one, listening to the Grand Canyon: "You don't catch the lambent X-rays, flamingo, wild 'cross palms' a-sigh-lum, Berkeley tarbaby's immortal gumdrop." Sara/ Justine, fingering kaballah mind-games, twinning & enwrapping corkscrew DNA evolving rebellion vibes of quietude, palimpisised themselves, disguised as lucid nobodies. Underwear tigers spoke thru a human-skull, politics in a wristwatch, jump listening, Grand Canyon's ear bicycling India to be at one, yea, they drove their winks, instant gathering, eternally put. All to bring Loraine to her novel synesthesia, heavy lamps were employed to bulldoze any skinny dreams they might intuit into an either/or. Finally, atop a witches-cradle, twirling geometries unblurred their neurological doorknob's compass to low & behold's apartment & wings swam into elbows of Archimedes. Crow-barring off the lid, vampiric funhouse mirrors arose, disappearing invisibility. Way down, mummified via too often tidings, Lorraine unwrapped herself, hip-hopping up the sticky walls of the chrysalis tomb. Scrolls imbued with kirlian images were lapped relay diplomas, epidermically printed

out for Kelsey's engram bank, from Lorraine mummification. "This rhymes one time only" Justine vibed to Sara, bathing her UFO immunology. The mother egg-ship quieted now that Lorraine was safely in harness, so one listening to their pendulum heartbeats synchronize, galloped away any singularity left. They became total formalists waiting for the outside upset, seeking the perfect avoidance, the blissful abyss, nirvana's oblivion. Different rivers of duration commingling olamic-always guttered into simulacrum nostrils of King Cobras umbrellaing off night's energy until atomically neutral makings wanted to be the origin of their source. Daphne cracked the womb-door of her meditating awareness. "Nothings ever done with." She announced. "Benign insanity is waking everyone toward delight's enchantment", Kelsey replied, as she took the controls off automatic pilot, opened a portal & pushed her nipples into the nighttime's branching warp-speed, as the mythical Jell-O that enfolded them & reified every here into a now of beginnings' always, wiggled realities' event.. Sara & Justine quickly dragged their pilot away from the suck of the dark hole. When they laid her down unconscious on the revolving I floor, Kelsey's body flashed a pulsing code Daphne could read. "Turn left & join eternity", it said. Yet, there being no one the crew could follow, delay & mayhem ensued. Questions arose stymieing their general will. Was Daphne's translation a perfect mirror of the code? If so, how do we interpret it's meaning? Is the code a parable, a metaphor or to be taken literally? Who or what send it? Fears came up. " We don't know whether this message we've received is an attempt to draw us into a trap or happy freedom", Sara posited, amid the wild flaying of arms, loose from their usual oar-handles. After slapping the cheeks of Kelsey, Justine tried to stand her up with the aid of Loraine & Daphne, but their captain was limp as a paraplegic beanbag. "Let's take a vote on what to do & I'll umbilical myself out into original neutrality in case I'm the only dissenting one", Justine proposed.. No delete must quit, he thought, from everything here, to escape us into clarity. The survival instinct unrolled comeuppance in Loraine like the opening fern tip of beginning's green creation, pointing her attention toward an angel creature beating its wings inside an iceberg that floated by within some estranged meta-mind she recalled, when this acting moment had supervened, rising its tree of remembrance. Both diaphanous & nevertheless seen, outlined around a void that made this eidolon up, by her feelings of no recognized sense, waving appendages drew all Loraine's thoughts into this passing jewel of mazes' insight. Then, her bones became echoes, jungle geometries, a walking slime mold, contingently meandering in slow desperation for the ichor of fat light. Her habiliment evaporated into a mist that fell back icy pinpricks condensing to dewy amour & then smithereening again, becoming one vaporous poltergeist rising & taking over with the barbwire stars caging all known mythical imagination, so that from this put-on-hermeneutics' take-off, Loraine novelty knew, a priori, the coming doom of every sheltered universe. Horror vacuums whizzed by, suicidal other-worlds gestured come-ons in the apertures of unique life. "I am your original bias", Gaza announced, yet noticing this objectified nobody at the brainstorm which dancing quantum-jumps like an amphetamine flea, jitterbugged their vibe into one quaking zoom. The ship's voice added: "We colossal intimacies have been stumped by our own minds which have no mind of their own". Sara, Daphne & Justine, who had folded their bodies into lotuses & ensconced themselves within an eggshell of quietude, were so humpty-dumptyed by the craft's outburst & jig, they became wild-eyed lighthouses with legs blindly running into each other, over & over again until their whirling kaleidoscopic visions jelled in an arresting episteme & the three froze in a mutual hypnotic trance. After a minuet by Loraine, first Sara woke, then Daphne & finally Justine, sans any membering remembrance of their flip-out, each examining their bruises & yowling a little, they harnessed themselves & took up the oars. Loraine, afraid to relate, what had ensued, less, the powerful truth of what she knew would further debilitate the mother-ship's necessary crew, like Plato, kind of nobly lied. "There was a rogue wave shakeup, that I guess knocked you all out." Telling her self that gerrymandered creative Irish truths make the always possible, since everything we absolutely invent is a tomb that can't be opened to even know what passed finally now, as they entered ghost-clouds, silver pleading-faces of one's dear dear ones whispering through the thoughts of every mind: "Let me in, it's sheol to be haunted by myself." Kenning that all their p-300 waves, commingling equally tunes of logic & emotion unto feeling/thought, were flooding them with ubiquity gestalts & that she & these erstwhile crew members as an ensemble had the why/what/where/how and who stance to guide their always, toward happy freedom, Kelsey instantly curling up for a distance-run, joining them, just one more added impossible nonsense, relinquished, sans a blue-print, her leadership & the path opened onto a new giant wheee.

As The Way Out Is In & The Way In Is Out-Of-Sight

OT WANTING or needing to disturb ancient ecology, except for the asleep bugs, mineral spirits, rhizomes, unknown living etc.. I dug a home with Tosca's help. Zombie machines & golem dung-beetles pushed the dirt from the carefully sculptured corridors that wended around the tendrils (seeking their rare grail). Only when inside the immense living room theatre were they or anyone for that matter able to goof with truth. Illumination was mostly supplied via reflective tunnels running to the daylight or moonshine & star-twinkle surface. The other brightness needed came from electric transparent deep-sea creatures, trapped & released on my diving-bell dips, giving them a vacation in another world. These see-thru creatures may be unveiled in their pressurized fish-bowls as I just did to write this to all reading disciples of THE ANTI-SLAVERY & PRO-INTELLIGENCE PARTY. Every tenth night, following Tosca's blueprint, we would stitch up Frankensteins out of nano-fibers into buttery diplomats, who could muster approval from the living golems, zombies & go-alongs that were prevalent above, so they wouldn't be lead to entomb us & the other undergrounds inhabiting this dear yird. Sociopath corporate types, either at the top ring of or angling for the upstairs' merry-go-round of their icy heaven, puppeteered those capable of questioning into imaginations kept within whatever game-rules maintained by the abacus-brain status quo. Doing all the step-&-fetch-it, wage slaves serviced these elite populists, who ran about, too, under the illusion of bettering themselves while helping the disadvantaged. Among these ills & evils of imbalance, from lack personal responsibility, victim ideologies grew demanding to be cradled throughout theirs lives via their government & the church. Sharking cynicism also flooded the land: "if you're so smart why ain't you rich", "Do them before they do you", so that any one with any feeling/thought whatever either closed it down or weeping silently within, blamed themselves for their lack of merit to get ahead. Therefore, our underground needed to cabal the easily taken in, so they by their will-less-will would distract the anti-empathics away from looking down to far & deep out. That is until one day I overheard, while visiting near the surface, a voice talking to itself, as bedraggled figures toiled with their 'goods' up a distant hill, "….just to keep their mind on the road even when you're wheeling thru God's brain" & I knew this Thin' (as we called

those above ground) not only gave to each their own, moreover, was also teaching other 'Thins' the in-between. I called up to him from the hidden tunnel & the man jumped back in astonishment as if the bush covering the entrance, spoke. Parting the branches of the plant & thrusting my face out, I entreated: " we live under here, come & join us. Don't be afraid, Tosca & I would enjoy the company of the first intelligent humanoid residing above, we've met in decades". Still hesitant, I thought because this Juniper bush might have a physiognomy, I pulled myself completely out of its twiggy grasp & standing fully before what I hoped would be at last a peer living among the 'Thins' with whom we, of the empathic underground could meet & exchange tales, I suppose, mostly of woe, yet, perhaps, via this sharing, lift our resolve to emerge anywhere greeted by just friends, I held out my hand. He, after a moment to ken my vibes, clasped my arm with both his palms & embraced me. Then, since my new-found wise 'Thin' looked anxiously about as if our meeting would bring dire trouble upon us, I quickly escorted him into our underground haven. Tosca, who never visited & only rarely, from our tunnels, peeked up at the above world & was even flighty among our deep clan whenever vibes were raised, took immediately to this quiet, calm stranger as he emerged into the living room of our earthen home. So much so, that even though I am not a possessive person by nature & believe that ownership even of the inert was an untoward illusion, a longing for my familiar's meditative company arose like a sweet ache within me. They spent hours together, soul diving into each others eyes, mindful of all, it seemed, yet oblivious to any salient particular, except the living darkness within them. We, as a practice & by now by nature, never spoke under here, unless such an address would be required for anyone's immediate survival. With Tosca's continual guidance, the stranger, after a few days of mumbling to himself, adapted to our silent act. Yet, when she saw he could express his communiqués without words & began turning her healing & friendly attention more & more to herself & others ailing of understanding, who needed the gift of her presence & focus, the man-from-above, at first, on Tosca's 'rounds' & meanderings through the halls & cathedrals of our dig, just tagging along by her side or trailing behind her like a giant hungry puppy dog, became, whenever she was away from him for one moment, an out-of-control helicopter, flailing his winged limbs about until he 'crashed' on the earthen floor, limbs still jumping out in gestures' dying kick. Tosca & I, with our fellow 'undergrounder',

Star Velvet, tried serenade our ailing inhabitant into a balancing calm, but our numinous melodies could not enter his feeling-mind. "I must have you" the stranger called out to Tosca, when she passed by him, affrighting her into deep withdrawal. So, because of this speech act & since we failed appeasing & liberating this obsessed soul, he, in turn, having upset the living vibes of not only Tosca, but each us considerably, I lifted my reluctant humanoid, biting my arms as we went, up to the surface. Even after our visiting Stranger was sadly taken away by the 'Thins' medical officialdom, I Lingered awhile at the top, wondering if we of the 'below' were not the delusional ones eschewing all human conversation. Maybe a talking-cure would have drawn him out of his womb/tomb enrapture? I was about to descend, when the sky glowed & I heard muffled explosions. Thins poured over the hills toward me carrying banners & signs too distant to decipher. Wanting to find out what was happening, I held my ground like an anchored stone in a rushing current as they swiftly passed by me with their fluttering placards. I couldn't read one sign. Even the letters were alien. Finely out of nescient desperation, I tackled one of the fleeing 'Thins' & carried her, kicking & pounding on me all the way, down into Earth Star, our dugout home. Tosca, upon hearing the girl's shrieks echoing through the tunnel, rappelled her self way beneath us, where the lungs of fiery breathing whooshed up a soothing mist that evanesced all high desire to lord over another. Placing the young woman 'Thin' in a featherbeded room & inundating her senses with salubrious experiences, she calmed & quieted down in ten days. Root-a-toot instructed her in our gesture alphabet & the caring principals we lived by as best we could. "People are awaking to individual & social responsibility" Nim, the name we gave her, signworded to us, "which has aroused fear in some who feel their lives are held together by what has been & is now not holding. The old ideas & practices of individuality, freedom, private-property, ownership, power, hierarchy, citizenship, economics, democracy, religion, medicine, education, nationhood & our relationship with the cosmos & other living creatures are not only being questioned, they are no longer operative with a growing number of people! That's why I was so resistant when you grabbed me. I thought you were the establishment fuzz". She paused for a moment to catch our response. Star Velvet spoke up in charade language: "Now that you know the way we live by down here, what critique would you give?" Nim cocked her head like a robin seeking a possible worm. "Well, I congratulate you for escaping the unfeeling thoroughfares & heart-rendering victimhood ' society' that only a con-scienceless intellect & its go-a-longs thrives in, however, each one of you faces the question of whether to dig deeper into the netherworld, remain in your cave here or emerge & join the alive inertia of the growing resistance & social/personal creativity above". She paused again waiting for a further response. "I am willing to learn the common written languages of the 'Thins' if you will teach me", came a gesturing from Root-a-toot. "Yes, I will be your Janus deity of exits & entrances, a lift between the upstairs & downstairs, until the real social in-between happens between us all". So, from then on, Nim would pop in & out of the tunnels, as some of us of the underground dug deeper to escape the public cries & nurture our individual souls & some arose to join the 'Thin' s resistance. Yet, I feel, as I now, hidden by the Mul-berry bush, peek in & out at the light & darkness within & without from this twi-light perspective, that either way, no way, both/&/or new ways, one ventures, respecting the sensitivity of each such, is bringing about a 'good, great, beautiful & free' cosmos.

RACING MISS DAISY

MARIE HIPPITY-HOPPED across the feldspar commons as she x-rayed thru her shifting-shape: zazen hum-a-bobbas. These were characters recalled & made-up in dreamlife. Aging had been solved, so there, of course, were less & less people to know, just the same growing younger & older (the role-sliders) & the same (flesh-trances) hanging on to ideal periods of their remembered existence. Without this imagining ability, I'd be caught networks eternal doldrumed set-theory reunion, tap-danced within blinking eyelids, lighthoused in her lonely cranium, public-signaling we could all know. Who was ahead of what in the race between the why & the how, kline-bottled thru its no-escape. The mineral spirits, hydrogen, helium & thy urchin: lithium, informed trinity phalanxes against tohu-bohu, stirring-up invented ambrosia from our beginning's hello. Caldrons of slow-fire banked longevity embers' unendingly dash into readymade apocalypse, though, just a light near around the globe that never came. Instead, this magic fearless sphere, within membrane questions riddled with puzzles' enigma, gulped its hidden-skin, imprisoned there, by an everlasting wall of holy geometry we may climb or descend, yet, she whizzed over & under, always growing thought-structures, intuitive awareness butterflying hands upon golden wheelie's thermostat, radaring inhibited pop-sickles. Lazy ghosts drank sundown. Mist tickled her olive-leaf aura commingling with nightfall rising urban pyre-shadows glancing thru arroyos, beams of dusty cries off exhausted havoc-gas. Jupiter hospitable pilgrims sauntering ocean knapsack giant creeper toes pointed to infinite varieties' lay-away nosecone, stealing by doily curbs, incoming kiss, waving indexicals edgewise. Maries, reemerged from her omni-jeep, so mimicked in presence-vibes, one couldn't differ with another. There was no violence, in fact, no one wanted the chance of a unique unease even. Ecological busybodies tattletaleing on the peacefully-scared haunting in media res, cussing, out-of-focus, 'swear with your wits', echoed from her inner-world, as the between & outside gave her aesthetic pain, zubzwang non-locality cradled this miss upon the teasing flow. Everything that wasn't a thing, pioneering valences, embracing undefined otherness, wiffling-whew, calcining howdah, dawking mickyfinn tweetybirds, again, inhibited death's lollypop, climbed way-down into around flying on spin-rads, dervishing all polarities, whizzy-quiz & quantum-language recording oracle's U-turn NONAME & EVERYWHERE. 'He wasn't running for

57

smack, but it may come to that', Noname thought, limbs drumming under him, whiling goodbye, eyeing through branches reaching above, intriguing to climb, wresting swimming-pools held in common, being impossible, this is my juice, a unique mix-up, fluttering identities' picture-show, dreaming never-ending tales arising before now, desperate everywhichway caught within fiery glows' smooth nerve, unrepeated rhymes coming around in infinite longings, hugging a beginning & end that never touch, perfect circling indiscovented from alive remakes like a heisinberg orgasm, walking metronomes' tomato-fork, Noname gripped Everywhere's doorknob, hesitant, listening, then pushed until a thin slanted light-ray falling over his corduroy shoe, widened, enveloping him. This door opened onto a luminous mild sea hiccupping underneath his feet, knife-points seemed to be tickling him forward, geometry bubbling electron-vectors drew him too. Gatherings of any kind were slightly repelled by his inability to identify with either them or himself, even though an averaging he couldn't understand forced Noname to join, ala' Groucho Marx, the very unconscious gang that wouldn't have him, becoming always lost in solitary crowds of mars-bar appointments hanging around butter-finger taxicabs with nothing left but free-jive. 'Where is her apartment?' This Rumi, ruminated. 'Everything I imagine must be real on some obscure leveling nirvana-dishevelment or maybe a paralleling bridged your flying-on when the extremeophiles are widening-away spiritual unions. Do minds so full of loving the beloved see clearly, lucid as Descartes?' He doubted nega-tiva even. Noname finely espied her retinue surrounding Everywhere, passing before him this lioness angel, flowing like the desert-dunes, quick & slow to the mood of the whimsical breezes, yet guided by a lodestone that shone upon all bedazzled wavy-knaves, entouraged in principled arms, giddy-upply jounced. Before Noname could announce himself, trumpets blew the royal blues inhered with the destiny of a zillion wailing trains & forlorn steam-whistles, drowning out the oming unfinished sea within him, heavens jostling cradled globes' whiffenpoof mind, bringing the new-now to his immediate awareness, then, silence comes out & palimpsest elevators deep in inner-space, baton at once, wild glimpses, rainbow-arching over froggy climbs of Notre-Dame. 'Smithereening into arabesque pin-cushions, black-pansy vases, containing & releasing the jinni of late-eve's dwelling, almost strangled with ivy, rooted via life's grinning anchor, keeping this emotional bankbook afloat, you don't have to shot-putt diving-bells', he thought, as a shout rang out of him: "You knock my coconuts", naming him forever: Hereabouts.

HeShe Visitation

"ONCE FLOODS eye-droppered & hurricanes tornadoed a hole-in-one, before the first Sun red-dwarfed & expanded, blitzkrieging everything on earth into a donald duck sand dune, every survival idea was pounced upon like a piece of meat to a famished lion. That's because we didn't know everything & nothing would break-dance & then pool its spin into the omega unitarity." So jived Billy Prunepit's floating notions with an Inkling. "All our matter squeezed into an acceleration that left not even nothing lost. I was cool & airy with this, to say the breezy least, however, now, in my novel canoeing thought-forms, many not my own, my quantum memories are no longer looking for & from initial truth, they want to extend & deepen yonder beyond their pollywogging imponderance, their slippery consciousness & be an added sense." A Rorschach erupted from Billy's purpling companion: "You're the pure one who can't be mixed, I'm the mixed plurality that may become a pure one, that's what I behold at this nowistic angle." "No, you tergiversate me incorrectly, Inkling, I'm not a perfect that all can enter, nevertheless, while the apex shapes machined original dreams dreaming me & still blurred as a humming bird, I could look at my own mind nestled in the oceaning sky, kissing the recursive curls that never quite returned, I was happily cool, one might almost say in the newness off this neutrality, an absolute liberal. The Inkling intercomed in: "Minus a personal subjective eternity, of course!" "Yup, Intimate Shadow, membering astonishment & wonder replaced remembrance with internecine individual nows that grew oblivious to the anti-entropy falling upon the void, opening disappearance, tunneling diamond death, beckoning forth baby universes, origamiing space, until distancing smalled our suns coming upon us like peeled cantaloupes rolled off lava tongues' burning diving board, spheres flaming infinities into the endless blue." There was a pause here as a bright point golfed across their backdrop. "These doctoring skeletons don't help either" Little Night-Time mothered forth, "roboting logical catwalks as a safety net just become a webbing that distracts our meta-mind's touch of awareness, I suppose." "O Inkado, if you only knew, the touch touching touch of that old soul Being, fingering from a transcendental horizon, caterwauling me on & out of my lucubration, the virgin nausea I'm waved by, you wouldn't mention any outside intelligence of any kind, especially an umbrella one. I don't know about nor can I speak for you, yet, iridescent up-close, quoting a raven coal miner's son "but me no buts, sayeth the lord", I'm under the thumb of nobody. An unborn reproducing misplaced the auto-catalytic, nanoing tachylons, so calculations are no longer kung-fued by elite's gantlet. The Dark Winking interjected here: "they never were, no total alembic has been taking place, nor membranes precluding the becoming of everyone, our ones weren't islanded factoid dots making the watching picture of God. Yes, bungling ideology conspirators arrived on the right/left scene unfurling their wooly mind-flags, blindfolding us to the lost ground of our own grinding & once forever with the media & meme earthquakes & tsunamis blown out of proportion, tooled us as dragons of armored tears yet never wisdoming their clichés, they made more than a biomass hiccup really, everybody unbelieved in the post-belief era & that quantum membering was all we needed & now these business-bodies are, if they are our at all, doing nothing but reincarnating the upholstery of Gurdjieffs shoeshine stand." Billy was only slightly rebuffed by the reply of his interlocutor & continued, though he deemed, while vibeing his response, a tiny buggy confusion in his enlightenment as if he was mistaking hairs for letters & being led inexorably into a Venus Flytrap by his own one-way words: "It's my dingdong anyway reproducing spacecraft that eject launches upon only flying ideas steadying toward worm-hole bird-lands side-kicking a mouse-driven owl." "Don't you miss", the Inkling questioned, "the creak & thump along long-ago dusty paths' golden warmth & easy-going wooden towns?" Billy Prunepits looked into the night an eon it seemed & thought in an objective privacy necessary for at least enough coherence for him to understand himself: 'the Purple of the Purple is relatively correct in the magic of this flux, to her darkling I've been both alephed into the mystical silence around & throughout the panda bear of all unknown night & yet too, reduced to the small ancient bonzing carpenter, hammering mountain goats, springing up Egypts in an open sky-eye that never winks or blinks even.' A crazy magnet of envy & repulsion drew Billy through the osmosis of dreaming solids, past the vast rinky-dinks onto a saddling algorithm galloping galaxies after galaxies. Reading a whisper of smoke from their embering, the lost fact of his being akasically virgin in the hermit glove of their dazzlement, he listened to this listening, gone, he hoped, only in the eerie airlessness' twinkle of deep shebang.

www.ingramcontent.com/pod-product-compliance
Lightning Source LLC
Chambersburg PA
CBHW080818250626
47159CB00010B/3426